A HOME FOR SUMMER

TALL, DARK AND DRIVEN~BOOK FOUR

BARBARA DELEO

FANCY A FREE NOVELLA?

***Waiting on Forever**—Alex's story—is the prequel to my Tall, Dark and Driven series and is available **exclusively** and **free** for subscribers to my reader list.*

You can claim your free novella at the end of this book!

CHAPTER ONE
LESVOS ISLAND, GREECE

*H*ot tears pricked her eyes as Summer Adams bent to pick up the tiny pink bead lying among a pile of stones in a corner of the tumbledown room. As she held it between her thumb and forefinger, she gently blew away a film of dust to reveal flecks of gold and silver and gave in to the inevitable.

It was over. Finished. Her hopes of coming here, selling this wreck of a house, and finally being able to buy the home of her heart in Brentwood Bay had disintegrated.

She wasn't a resident here, and she didn't have enough money to renovate and sell. The laws of this village, this island, had wiped away all her hopes and dreams. Nausea curled in her belly, and the image of everyone she owed money to back home erupted in her mind; everyone who, like her, was waiting 'til she cracked the golden egg she'd promised was waiting for her on an island in Greece.

What a silly little fool.

As she squinted at the tiny sphere in her hand, a mash of rage, sorrow, and frustration bubbled deep within her. Turning to the broken window, she screwed her eyes tight and with all her strength threw the wretched, hateful, heart-breaking thing as far as she could.

But the pain and the wanting, the sadness and the anger it had sparked, stayed rooted inside her.

As her eyes flew open, a sob lodged in her throat. In a panic, and imagining another part of her mother lost forever, she pushed on the latch of the sagging door to the lane, desperate to get outside and retrieve the bead.

It wouldn't budge. Of course it wouldn't. Maybe it was a sign, maybe—

"Hello?"

Lurching back at the shock of a voice from the window, her heart somersaulted as a face poked through. Sleek black waves of hair framed an angular face, and dark glasses sat on a regal nose. Skin the color of dusk covered the plane of a firm jaw and sat smoothly across unforgettable cheekbones. The entire, manly vision caused breath to stall in her throat.

"Is this yours?" His voice was powerful and slow. "Or someone else's unguided missile?"

Her pulse skipped at the tone of his rich Greek accent, and she took an involuntary step back. To have anyone walk down the lane in this island village seemed enough of an event. The fact he spoke English and looked like her teenage impression of a Greek god was way too good to be true.

"I'm so sorry," she finally said, warmth spreading across her cheeks as she tried to still the rhythm in her chest. She dusted her hands on her denim shorts. "Did it hit you? I was...cleaning up...it sort of...slipped."

Was he angry or amused? The heavy set of his brow and the unforgiving line of his perfect mouth gave nothing away, so she spoke to fill the silence. "I've been here for at least an hour, and I'm sure nobody's walked past. I thought this part of the village must be deserted."

Leaning a strong muscle-bound forearm on the wooden

sill, he held the bead through the window. It sat pretty and fragile in his large hand as he spoke. "Not deserted. People are having their siesta. But not me. I was coming to see you. If you're Summer."

"Ahhh," Summer stuttered, "yes, yes it...achoooo!!" Her lungs pulled tight as she gasped for air.

"Bless you," he said, with the tiniest twitch of his mouth.

"Asthma." Summer rasped as she reached for the gray inhaler in her back pocket. After breathing the medicine deep into her lungs, she managed to say, "All this...dust."

"I can see. Have you been stirring it up since yesterday?"

As he spoke, she imagined what sort of eyes were behind those glasses, eyes that might probe and explore her inner-most desires, crack the shell of confidence she'd been trying to hold so carefully around herself ever since she'd arrived.

"I was supposed to meet you yesterday but was delayed, and I didn't get to the island until late last night. I had some other work to do this morning."

"Kirieh...Nicoliedies, is it?" Summer said, her tongue tripping over the name. She knew she was murdering the Greek words, but her lips tightened. "My mother's lawyer in California said I should expect you sometime yesterday." He might be pissed that he'd had to come looking for her, but at least she hadn't been the one who'd missed their meeting.

He transferred the bead to his left hand and held out his right. "Costa."

Placing her own hand in the broad palm offered, she immediately felt the strength of him as a shiver began where they joined and swept up her arm.

He spoke as if those around him always listened, the smooth planes of his face held in a way that indicated assur-ance and mystery. "I'm Costa Nicoliedies."

The dark glasses unnerved her. Like a model in an ad for aftershave, he exuded indifference and attitude. She slid her hand from his grip, already missing his strength, and took a step back.

"Costa? Oh, I'm sorry, I must've heard your name wrong yesterday. Of course, that's one of my biggest problems in being here, I don't speak Greek."

"It doesn't matter." An upward movement in his lips, but not quite a smile. "I'm sure you'll get by."

"I'd invite you in, but…" She finally stepped forward again to take the bead. A moment's hesitation as her hand floated above his, and she tried desperately to control the nerve endings that were firing at random.

He didn't pass the bead to her but held it flat in his palm. Waiting.

Like a bird collecting its prey, she plucked it away, shoved it into the pocket of her shorts, and again stepped backward, out of the ring of confidence that surrounded him.

"I can't open the door. I came through the basement."

"No problem." Costa gripped the top of the window frame, his biceps bunching as he vaulted effortlessly through.

The black T-shirt he wore defined the dark brown of his skin. It must be every girl's fantasy to have a muscled Greek man leaping through her window, but Summer wasn't quite sure how she felt about someone being so…forward. Right at this moment, though, he was her last hope to turn this situation around.

"I'm in now." He stretched his lithe frame, as if he'd completed the Olympic pole vault, then shot her a heart-stopping grin.

"So you are." Heat rushed to her face as his presence dominated the small space. She reached for the jade tiki that lay at her throat and smoothed the cool green stone under her fingers. She was far more comfortable when people kept their distance, not so near she could feel their warmth.

Costa pulled off the glasses and carefully folded them. His

striking eyes now unveiled, the polished coal pupils drew her in—dark, mysterious eyes that could make you forget your own name.

"What can I do for you?" he asked. "This looks like quite a project."

Now she knew where that confidence began, she couldn't drag her gaze away and held the pendant tighter.

"Well," she said, struggling to bring her attention back to her immediate problem, "I need your help to find a way around the island's laws. I have to get this place ready to sell, but the authorities won't let me."

"What do you mean?" His gaze swept around the room before settling on her again. "I was told you needed someone to help translate while you sold the house. No one suggested selling could be a problem."

"I'm not *allowed* to sell it." Her throat constricted again at the memory of the news she'd been given yesterday. "The person from the island's housing authority I spoke to said that, as a foreigner, the only way I can renovate property to sell is if I can give proof of funds from a bank account in my name."

He fixed her with a stare, as if to ask why on earth that would be a problem.

"If you knew me," she said as she pulled the bead from her pocket again, "you'd understand that's about as likely as this little thing finding its way back to the string it came off."

Costa folded his arms in front and leaned back against the wall, his face creasing in confusion. "You came here expecting to renovate and sell the house without checking out the island's property laws first?" His tall frame reached most of the way up the wall.

The awful logic of his question caused her stomach to clench all over again. "I've never been here before. Had no idea what to expect. My mom left me the house, so I just assumed I could come here and sell it, but when I arrived, I found it was in this state." She waved her arm to show the chaos that surrounded them. "My mom's lawyer never mentioned it might be so run down, or that selling it could be this complicated. If I'd known, maybe I wouldn't have—"

"And the housing authority immigration officials won't let you renovate or sell as a foreigner?" He looked down at the packed earth floor and smoothed it with an expensive-looking boot. Despite his cool smiles, something simmered beneath the polite facade. Maybe he didn't want to be here, didn't want to help. Not her, not now.

"No, they won't. Apparently, they've had people start to renovate and give up halfway through, leaving a bigger mess than when they started." She lifted her chin. "It's just a hideously vicious circle. I'm depending on a sale because I really need the money to close on a house back home, but I can't sell this place because I don't have the money to renovate." Silence stretched between them until she spoke again. "What were you expecting to do here before all this?"

He looked up, his gaze more intense, reeling her in. "Your mother's lawyer was looking for someone to help with translation for sale deeds. I was coming back for a few weeks so I said I'd help, but I wasn't expecting this. What is it you need?"

Her pulse fluttered at the change in his eyes. What did she need? To get out of this house, this village, this country on the other side of the world. To get back home so she could finally pay for the house in Brentwood Bay that was slipping from her grasp.

It was so typical of her mother, springing another surprise on her. To not even tell Summer before she'd died that she had a house in Greece, let alone that it was in this state...Even from the grave, she seemed intent on dragging

6

Summer from one place to the next. Hurt and sorrow and cold, bald grief clung together inside her.

"I've only been on the island for two days." She tried to disguise the wobble in her voice. "I spent all of yesterday in a town about an hour away, only to eventually be told by the housing authority that even if I had the money in the bank, I couldn't sell until the house was habitable and met their specifications." Her lungs tightened again at the thought of renovating this dust heap.

"This is the old part of the village, and it comes under a presidential decree as being a traditional village of outstanding beauty." His gaze washed over her while he spoke. "There are strict rules here on Lesvos about what you can do to the houses. My father's the mayor of the area. He feels very strongly about things like this. The island authorities have no option but to enforce those rules."

She nodded as he repeated what she'd been told yesterday. And it made sense—from everyone's viewpoint but hers.

Costa's dark eyes scanned the room, then landed directly back on her. "So, what's the problem? Can't you just get a loan back home and then renovate? Pay it back when you've got the proceeds of the sale?"

"No." Her heart squeezed tighter. "My bank and I aren't seeing eye to eye right now. A loan's impossible."

How could she get out of this mess without telling him her complete life story? That she'd poured every cent she could scrape together into a house deposit so she could take care of her mom in the time she'd had left. That she'd held down three jobs to save for her mom's medication. None of that had turned out the way she'd planned, and it looked like none of this would either. "I've got very little money right now. I had to borrow from a friend to buy the plane ticket to get here, and I only have enough left for a couple nights' accommodation. Finding the house like this was all so...unexpected."

"I see."

But he didn't see, and that was the problem. His voice had hardened, and he seemed thrown by what she'd said. He stood against the wall, a picture of irritation, while her dream turned rapidly into a nightmare.

"You were told you had no other option than to prove you have money before you renovate?"

She sighed. "As a foreigner? Absolutely none. The man yesterday said that anyone who wants to renovate in a protected village in Greece must follow very special rules, and the rules for foreigners state they must show they can carry the renovation to completion. And for that they need money."

How she wished she could get on and do this all herself. Why couldn't her mother have had a house in Australia or England? She must have had money to buy this place, another gift from Summer's generous grandparents she suspected—the grandparents Summer had never met because her mother had cut all ties before Summer's birth. As usual, her mother had decided for her, assuming that her own roaming way of life—owning nothing and staying nowhere for long, no home or family—would suit her daughter.

"Yes, the rules for foreigners are different in a case like this." His eyes narrowed a fraction. And was that a slight nod? As if he'd been chewing her situation over and suddenly found a solution?

Was it possible he could help her? Was there a chance he could find a way to bend the rules so she could at least get the house ready to sell? Her heart quickened with the hope of it.

"So, you'd intended to stay in the house before you sold it?" he finally asked.

"I was hoping to, at least until I had a buyer. I've done plenty of travel before in the States but never overseas. I guess, I guess I was just too..." Her hands did the flapping thing that made her feel less out of control, but the treacherous burn of tears stalled her words.

Costa seemed unsettled by her sudden display of emotion and pulled his lips a little tighter. "That's a decent set of issues to deal with. How bad is your asthma?"

She took a big breath in through her nose. "Not bad. As long as I'm not stressed out and surrounded by dust all day. I was hoping," she continued, mentally crossing her fingers, "that you might talk to the council for me, ask them if they'll make an exception. Explain that, although I don't have the money right now, I really have to sell this place."

This was torturous, asking a complete stranger, a completely *gorgeous* stranger, for help, but she had no choice. Either she walked away now and lost all hope of paying off her debts, or she could find a way to sell this house and have the life she'd always imagined. To finally have a home at last. A home nobody could take from her.

His cool, searching stare pinned her again, and this time she wished she'd said nothing. "But you'd still need money to renovate."

A bead of sweat tumbled down her back. She couldn't speak the language, couldn't meet the requirements to sell the house, and had absolutely no money. Her gaze darted away from the hold his stare had on her. She wanted to escape the flutter in her chest that began each time she waited for him to speak.

The effort to control her emotions saw another rogue sigh escape her lips. Why would a complete stranger care about helping her bend the rules? And the son of the mayor at that? It was clear by the way he looked at her, all cool and calm, that he wasn't going to say what she needed to hear. Closing her eyes, she sucked a defensive breath in the second before he spoke the words that would surely end her dream.

"There's no way I can help you bend an island law," he said. "It's there for a good reason—to ensure people renovate properly, that the traditions and atmosphere of the village are protected. We can't have people coming in and putting up plastic fences and multicolored roofing tiles. We also can't have people start something when they have no capacity to complete it. Also, our tradespeople need to know they won't be left empty-handed or worse when some dreamer skips the country."

Some dreamer.

Is that what he thought of her? Her eyes opened, and for the first time she noticed tiny hints of gray in his otherwise jet-black hair. His tight and toned physique suggested youth, but the silvery streaks, maturity. He was definitely in his late thirties. "Then there's nothing I can do but walk away," she said, again feeling the prickle of backed up tears. "I have no money. I just wanted to sell this...thing...so I could take some money home and...start again."

Costa walked around the room. He was tall, his spine ramrod straight and his chin a fraction higher than was natural.

He stopped and slapped the palm of his hand on one wall, making her jump. "Most of it seems quite solid, apart from a few places where water's got in. That's why some of the brick and stone have crumbled away. It leaves plenty of dust, but really it just needs to be re-packed and plastered. Wouldn't take long. Our local tradespeople are very experienced at this work."

He made it sound so simple.

"What's through here?"

Before she could answer, he moved to go through to the next room. He stopped at the door and pushed with a powerful shoulder, but it was stuck fast, leaving only enough of a gap to squeeze through.

Frowning slightly that he'd helped himself but glad he seemed more interested, she followed. Maybe he knew a way around the law—why else would he still be here?

This room was like the first, although a little smaller. One window, again with no glass, looked out on an orange grove that ran down a small hill. The sweet tang of orange, mixed with the soft scent of packed earth, filled the room. In one corner stood an old brick construction with an iron door in the center—some sort of fireplace beside a bathtub.

Costa moved toward it, his eyes growing wider as a warm smile lit his face. "I haven't seen one of these for years," he said, his hand on the brick top. His voice was suddenly lighter, excited even. "In the old days, you'd have to light a fire in here to get hot water." He touched an old faucet that sat over the bath. "My grandparents had one. They used the hot water for washing clothes...or themselves."

Summer sighed. She could imagine her mom here in the nineties, with who knew how many other 'free thinkers', incense burning, lounging about all day in the bath, and singing about peace, love and understanding.

Costa turned to face her and leaned back against the fireplace as a mysterious look flitted across his face. "What if I was to say there *is* a way around this, a way for you to renovate legally and sell before you leave the country?"

Blood rushed to her core and Summer gave up a silent vote of thanks for whoever had sent her this wonderful man. "I'd say I'll do whatever it takes," she said, unable to stop the smile that pushed its way across her face. "Tell me—"

He held up a hand. "First, I need to know how long you've got."

For a second she wanted to fall into his soul-searching eyes. Shaking her head, she took a step back. "What do you mean?"

"How long do you intend to stay in Greece?"

"Four weeks. That's all the time I've taken from work. I'd thought I could sell quickly, in which case I could've gone home sooner..."

A sudden scuffle in the ceiling directly above made her leap back, and she let out a small squeal at the thought something might fall on her.

"Looks as though someone likes living here," Costa said as they both looked up.

When he glanced back at her, his eyes softening, she could finally see a funny side to all this, and for the first time, she felt the warmth of his concern.

"I'll tell you what I'll do," he said. "I'm back in the village for about a month too. If you agree with my plan, I think we could get this finished easily in that time. I can't guarantee you're going to like my idea, though."

"Even if there is a way for me to renovate legally, I don't have the money to do it," Summer said in desperation. Was he offering to pay for the work himself? Surely not. She could never be beholden to someone like that.

"I can help you sort out a builder, a plasterer, and," he said, thumping the tap again, "maybe a plumber. It shouldn't take too long to make this place habitable."

She was grateful, of course she was, but it still didn't solve her two major problems: finding a way around the law and, if she managed that, finding money for the renovations. The thought that working every day with Costa could also be an enormous problem was almost enough to make her turn and run right now.

~

"So you can pay for it," Costa said as he watched the light shine behind her sparkling blue eyes, "I'm sure I can help you find a job or two around the village."

As he spoke, he attempted to hide the panic plowing through him. He'd made a promise to ensure Summer left the island with everything she'd come for, and he sure as hell wasn't going to renege on it. But he hadn't counted on this set of circumstances.

And he'd also promised that Summer would never find out who'd really sent him here.

She wasn't what he'd expected. Stunning, yes, with luminous eyes that drew him in. But he had to ignore that fact and the stirring it caused in him right from the get-go. He had a task to complete in as short a time as possible, and given the restrictions they were both under, the only solution to their problem was flashing neon in his head.

Although her mother, Caroline, had spoken of a materialistic girl searching for her place in the world, Costa could see parts of her mother in her. Long blonde hair fell softly around her shoulders, whereas her mother's hair had been short and spiky, but even though he was only a boy then, he could remember the same delicate features he saw now.

Summer wore shorts, revealing perfect legs. Quite a contrast to his hippy teacher with her flowing skirts. But it was the pendant that lay on the pale skin of her throat that reminded him of something Summer's mom might've treasured.

He and Caroline had reconnected about ten years ago when she'd seen him in a magazine and had got in touch through his agent. In the last few months of her illness he'd made sure to text or call her most days and had been devastated when her lawyer had called with the news that she'd died.

He thought back to the day when, as a boy, his entire class

and most of the village had gone down to the jetty to wave her goodbye, everyone in tears. He'd never forgotten her, and he'd always remembered what she'd taught him about life and the way to live it, as well as what he owed her. If it wasn't for Caroline Adams, he wouldn't have seen the incredible success he had in his life. She'd been a vibrant, carefree person, the opposite of the tightly coiled woman who stood in front of him now.

He didn't like secrets, but when Caroline explained she didn't have long to live, he'd promised her absolutely anything. He'd have paid for her treatment, sent money to make her as comfortable as possible, but she'd wanted none of that. When he asked her to name one thing he could do for her, she didn't hesitate. Knowing her daughter would have to travel to Greece to claim the house, Caroline had asked him to look out for her only child while she was here, insisting Summer mustn't know about their emails and texts and that he mustn't help her out financially. She made him swear on it. Apparently, her daughter was frighteningly independent.

Hopefully, it wouldn't take long, so that he could leave this place—this village that closed in on him—and get back to Switzerland and the life he belonged in as quickly as possible. It was important that his time here be kept secret, away from prying lenses and the crude questions the paparazzi would often fire at him. The villagers would hate it if the gossip-hungry hordes overran the place the way they did the last time he was here. He'd had to take a detour coming to the island yesterday when one particularly rabid journalist popped up at Athens airport.

There was one simple way around the island's renovation rule—but he couldn't imagine she'd agree to it.

"What sort of job could I do here to raise the money?" Summer asked, her small brow furrowing deeper. "I don't have a work permit to earn cash, but what if I could make something, do something in exchange?" Her eyes grew wider.

Not for the first time that day, Costa thought how unnecessarily difficult this was going to be. Caroline had insisted he mustn't give Summer money either—apparently Summer finding a solution to that issue would be part of her journey —but it would be so much easier if he did. Her body language—the folded arms, the permanent little frown— made it clear she didn't want to be here either.

"You could teach English," he said, picking up on her idea. "Most people can speak a bit, but they're always looking to improve for the tourists. I'm sure you could trade an hour or two for some plumbing, a conversation or two for some building. Maybe even help at the school."

Her head tilted a little to the side and he could sense her indecision as she stuttered, "Oh, I don't think I'd be...I wouldn't know how to *teach* someone."

Why was she so flustered? Her mother had been an inspirational teacher.

"I think you could," he said, fascinated by the way he could almost see the cogs working behind her bright blue eyes. She wanted a simple way out of this, but there was none. What they'd have to do was the last thing he'd choose, but he'd never go back on a promise.

"Do you think so?" For a second, calm seemed to cross her face, and for the first time, her gaze truly met his. Hope radiated from the blue depths of her eyes and something pulled tight in his chest.

Another scuffle in the roof.

Her gaze moved to the ceiling in obvious dread, the milky skin of her neck stretching.

Her face was pale and without makeup. A blonde fringe fell across her forehead, making her appear younger than he guessed she was. Her lips, pressed together right now, held promises he imagined stealing if the moment were right...

When her gaze turned back to him, her teeth were gritted and she let out a sigh as she pulled the small pink bead from her pocket. "So tell me, how do we get around this rule? I'm prepared to do whatever it takes to get this place saleable. What do I have to do to get started?"

Costa looked down at her, his pulse beginning to harden as the words fell from his mouth before he'd truly thought them through. It was crazy, and it was outrageous, but it was what he had to do to honor the memory of her mother.

"There's only one way," he said, as he looked up and watched her eyes widen. "All you have to do is marry me."

CHAPTER TWO

"*B*reathe. That's it, just breathe in...and...out."

Costa's voice was husky with concern, and all Summer could concentrate on was the warm weight of his palm firm on her back. She sat where she'd slumped on the cold, hard floor—her head between her knees.

Oh, boy, did she need to breathe! This was no asthma attack, but the way her lungs had imploded when he mentioned marriage as the solution to her problem had set the room spinning. Married? To a delicious...stranger? No way! In her dreams, maybe, but not in the cold, hard light of day and for all the wrong reasons.

Doing as he said, she gulped in fat lungfuls of air, all the while trying to still her sprinting heart.

"Are you okay?" he asked again, as she kept her gaze fixed on the floor, trying to work out what on earth she'd say next. "Do you need a doctor?"

She shook her head and took one final deep breath before scrabbling to her feet, her cheeks hot with a mixture of shock and embarrassment. "Water. Maybe some water?"

"We need to get you out of here." His hand rested on her

shoulder, the connection sure and steady, and she ordered the blood not to rush to her face again. "Where did you say the other door is?"

She pointed to the stairs heading out back, glad for an excuse not to say anything straight away, desperate to get things clear in her head before finishing their crazy conversation.

Emerging from the dark house into brilliant daylight, the view dazzled her. Beyond the house, and running down a hill, was a small orchard. She could smell oranges, and the silver gray trees were olives she guessed. The hollow call of a dove made the entire scene magical, and she wished for a surreal second that she was here with Costa for all the right reasons.

"Come this way." He guided her by the elbow as if she was a hospital patient. "If I remember right, there's a spring at the bottom of this hill."

They walked in silence through the trees, dry grass and twigs crunching under their feet, until they came to where a pipe jutted out of a bank and splashed water into a concrete tub.

"We have a few of these communal springs dotted throughout the village," he explained. Why was he so calm when she was still hyperventilating? "If you look down here at dusk, you'll see some of the old ladies filling water containers. Of course, they have running water in their houses, it's just an excuse for them to get together and chat."

She chanced a glance into his enigmatic, deep brown eyes and saw something flit across his face. Surely, nothing could be nicer than living in a close community where you had an excuse to talk to your neighbors. So why didn't he live here anymore?

"Drink," he said, and still silent, she cupped her hands and swallowed the cool water. Had he forgotten what he'd suggested back at the house? His tourist commentary suggested he went around asking random girls to marry him every day of the week.

"Better?" he finally asked as she came up for air.

"Thanks." She moved to sit under an orange tree, the gnarled trunk offering strength as her pulse hiked again. "Look, I know you came here expecting to have a job translating, and obviously you're disappointed that it won't be happening, but there's nothing else I can do about it. I know you were only joking back there, but it shows how completely impossible this situation is." Hopefully, she was hiding the disappointment and deep sense of failure leaching out of her. If only his solution had been realistic. "I'll book my tickets on the ferry out tonight."

He leaned against the corner of the tub and looked at her so intently she had to fight the urge to look away. "So you'll give up? Just like that. You won't even consider the solution I've given you? I wasn't joking."

"I'm not giving up." Her throat tightened, and she frowned at his accusation. "There's no logical solution to this."

"I've given you a solution. It mightn't be conventional, might seem pretty complicated legally, but it gets you what you want. Something you clearly need."

Her heart hollowed. "Being married to someone I don't even know isn't something I want. Marriage should be special, sacred, not something you only do as a means to an end." She dropped her voice. His concern for her was touching, and she hoped she wasn't insulting him. "Costa, I really appreciate your offer and can see you made it with the best of intentions, but why would you want to go through something so huge when you don't even know me?"

He paused as if considering her logic before he spoke. "As you said, I came back to the island to do a translating job for four weeks. If you go back home now, where does that leave me? Without the job I came here to do. It's in my interests to have you stay and sell the house so I get what I was expecting." Something passed across his face as he spoke, something that suggested he wasn't being completely honest.

She clasped her damp palms together. He was right. He had been expecting to come and work here for an entire month, but she couldn't be held responsible for what she'd found. Self-preservation kicked in. She wouldn't feel guilty. Not about this too.

"What were you going to do when you'd sold this place?" He spoke quietly, possibly because he could sense the disappointment of her broken dreams. Part of her wanted him to understand how hard this was.

"There's a house, back home in California, that I'd dreamed of buying. Well, more than dreamed. I worked really hard to save for a deposit on it and had the agreement drawn up, but then my mom died. Learning about this place and the possibility of selling it seemed like the answer to my prayers, but now I'm up for penalties and interest payments on that place if I can't see this through." Her voice was thicker than she'd intended.

"This house. It's something you'd dreamed of for a long time?"

How was it he seemed to know where to touch her with his questions? Even the warmth in his voice could make her stumble.

"Yes." She swallowed. "I've never owned a house before; we didn't even have our own home when I was a kid." Thoughts of her mother in this place, perhaps even sitting in this same orchard, stung. That a house, a home, had been here all along—crumbling and empty—confused her even more. Even when her mom's cancer was terminal, and she'd finally agreed to Summer buying a place where she could take care of her, even then she hadn't mentioned this place.

"Then why not live it?" Costa said, his eyes sparking. "Why not take this opportunity that's presented itself and do what it takes to think big, walk free, live your dream? You and I'd be doing nothing more than signing a contract, an agreement to see this renovation through to achieve what you really want in your life. And, at the end, we both get what we want."

She faltered. He made it sound so easy, logical, as if marriage was nothing more than a formal contract between two adults for mutual gain. It was impossible, of course.

He shrugged. "It's your decision."

The confident set of his mouth as he spoke made her anything but sure about what to do next. The thought of agreeing to his proposal and then spending time with this warm and mysterious man—as her husband—sent hopeful fingers of light through her chest before she was pulled up short by the reality; she didn't even know him!

"I need your answer by tomorrow." He took a step away from the tub as if to leave. "We could have the renovation finished within a month and then both have what we came here for. I'll be at the coffee shop in the square tomorrow at ten to hear what you've decided."

She stood, her head thumping, heart plummeting as she realized he was leaving. She didn't want him to go, didn't want to make this decision alone, but time and her options were running out fast.

A mess. An unholy mess that needs to be sorted as soon as possible.

Costa strode back up the hill to his father's house to retrieve his luggage before he moved into a hotel room. He nodded to villagers and greeted people as they passed him, but his mind was elsewhere. A group of women were standing at the top of a rise and talking behind their hands. They probably hated that he was back here, bringing unwanted attention to their village.

He thought back to his encounter with Summer. No wonder Caroline had wanted someone to watch over her daughter when she was in Greece. He couldn't believe that Summer had a) not bothered to look into the state of the house before she came racing over here and b) assumed she'd be able to flick off a historic building and hitch a ride on the next plane home.

No, that was too harsh.

It was clear she was deeply affected by her mom's death—and conflicted about the whole situation—so all of that was understandable at a time like this.

He'd hesitated when his treasured former teacher had asked him to keep an eye on her only child, but only for a second. And that was because he hadn't stayed on the island for any length of time in years. Truth was, he'd have walked over hot coals if Caroline had asked him to. She'd known she didn't have long left and that the only thing she had to leave her daughter was the house in Greece.

Caroline had taught him at the age of twelve about the incredible world beyond the island's shores, and that had been the catalyst for him leaving the island at eighteen, much to his father's disappointment. Since then, he'd worked hard to build a life he couldn't have dreamed of before Caroline's influence. A life of travel, shifting between his residences in Switzerland, Germany and Portugal, was what made him the most happy—never having expectations on him, never having to succumb to a life of settling down and being trapped in a community.

So it was ironic that now Caroline wouldn't let him use

any of his connections and wealth to help Summer solve her problems. He'd tried to reason with Caroline, had told her that if he just gave Summer the money for the house, then she wouldn't even need to leave the States. It had been typical of Caroline to reply that that wouldn't teach anyone anything.

What he knew was that he'd made a promise to Caroline Adams before she died, and he was going to see it through in the only way he could and in the quickest time possible. If he couldn't use his money, then marrying Summer was the only option, and he only hoped she'd see that too.

Opening the door to his father's house, he hesitated. What if she said no? What if she followed through on her statements about marriage being sacred, and what if she took the evening boat off the island? Where would that leave his promise? He wasn't used to people second-guessing him and wasn't about to fail at this first hurdle, and he would bet Summer wouldn't either.

"Hi Dad," he called. "I can check into the hotel now, so I've come to get my bag."

He heard his father moving in the kitchen before he came to stand in the doorway. "Why do you need to stay in a hotel?" A frown pulled his salt and pepper eyebrows lower as he wiped his hand on an apron. "What's wrong with the room you've had since you were born?"

"There's nothing at all wrong with it." They'd had this conversation several times this morning, and still his dad wanted him here. "I've told you. I have to be on conference calls with Australia this week, so I'll need to be up at all hours of the night. I don't want to disturb you." Or risk his dad being irritated by any paparazzi that might appear. It was also suffocating enough to be back in the village without having his father questioning him every day about when he was going to return for good and why he wasn't married yet.

23

Married. If Summer agreed with his plan, then his father might be about to get his wish—well, the second part of it at least. He'd have to tell his dad about getting married to Summer, but he was certain his father and the rest of the village wouldn't be surprised about him being with an American girl they'd never met. So many people had a distorted view of how he lived his life, but that suited him more often than not. They'd have to keep up a pretense of sincerity though, or Summer could lose the opportunity to finish and sell the house.

Another reminder of how carefully he was going to have to juggle things in the next few months if he was to carry out Caroline's wishes. People always had expectations of what he should do when he was on the island, and he wouldn't have a lot of free time if he was going to help Summer.

His father went back into the kitchen, and Costa picked up his bag. He thought back to the conversations he'd had with Summer today. There was something about her. A flash of determination that lit her eyes when she spoke about her future, a stiffening in her limbs as she fought to hold back her disappointment at what she'd found here.

He might not be able to pay Summer Adams' way out of this, but he wouldn't mind betting that she'd take him up on his offer. A small spark of excitement flared—married for four weeks.

Summer stood outside the busy coffee shop the next morning. Should she go in? She curled her fingers into fists, the sticky warmth on her palms somehow soothing her jittery limbs. Nothing frightened her more than entering a room when she knew no one. Except for seeing the stranger who'd proposed marriage yesterday.

Scanning the tables set outside under an enormous tree, she noticed the chairs of bright blue matched the shutters at the windows. The morning sun threw pockets of warmth, intensifying the earthy smell of work boots and freshly brewed coffee. Old men sat in groups, some playing backgammon, some just chatting and flicking the worry beads dangling from their fingers.

It could be the perfect postcard from Greece, if this wasn't all a complete nightmare.

"*Kafe?*"

The little old man in front of her had a pencil stuck behind his ear. His grizzled chin showed his age, but his bright eyes twinkled.

"*Neh.*" Shoot, had she just said "no" instead of the "yes" she'd intended? On the flight over, she'd tried to learn some Greek from an app on her phone, but she'd had little chance to practice. She nodded her head vigorously to reinforce her answer before he beamed, then hurried inside.

Glad to avoid the inside of the shop, she collapsed gratefully on the nearest chair, hoping she wouldn't have to wait too long for Costa. Feeling out of control, and not knowing what would happen next, had her mind flip-flopping and her body exhausted from a restless night's sleep.

She didn't trust what she was going to say to him, but after much soul-searching last night, it was clear his solution was the only one. No matter how much she wanted her first marriage to be born from the deepest love, this was the only way to move forward in her life, to allow her the freedom to make the right choices in her future. It had been four months since she'd paid the deposit on the house in Brentwood Bay. Two months since the promise to move her mom in and take care of her had been cut short by her mom's death. Now the bank back home was running out of patience and so was the realtor. If she didn't come up with the balance of the money, she could kiss the house and her credit rating goodbye. Walking away from a house sale here wasn't an option.

As she'd lain awake in her rented room last night, she couldn't stop thinking about Costa. How she was affected by his confidence, lulled by his certainty about everything, and overwhelmed by the way her body was drawn to him. He was older than her, maybe even by ten years. Was it his maturity and self-confidence that drew her to him? Whatever it was, mastering her emotions was key when she saw him today.

Shoving on a pair of plastic sunglasses, bought out of necessity at Athens airport, she looked out to the brilliant blue of the bay.

Had her mother ever sat in this spot? Smelled the warm sweetness of the olive trees? She'd never know. Her mother had never spoken about Greece, or if she had, Summer hadn't listened. Their entire life together had been a blur of moving from one town to the next, trying to make friends and find a place in the community only to be dragged somewhere else again. Dots on a map had meant upheaval and heartache, not the new beginning her mother had always promised for them.

The only place Summer had ever felt really at home was Brentwood Bay. Apparently, her mom had waitressed there in the months before Summer was born, and they'd occasionally go back for vacations. When she was eighteen and sick of their nomadic life, Summer had chosen Brentwood Bay as her base to study nursing and had stayed there ever since. It's where she would go back to when this was over. Where she'd build herself a real home.

The café owner came back carrying a pyramid-shaped tray with one small cup and one glass of water resting on the base. Summer bent down and reached into her bag for some money but, when a shadow crossed the sun, realized Costa was standing beside her. She paused for just a moment, hoping to still the wings that beat rapidly inside her chest. Slowly, she straightened.

"*Kirieh Nicoliedies!*" the old man exclaimed, slamming the tray on the table so the coffee splashed a crude brown stain on the small, white saucer.

Around them, chair legs scraped on cobbles as old men stood, exclaiming in equally loud voices as first one, then another, moved forward and thumped Costa on the back. Some even pulled off their black felt hats as they drew closer to shake his hand.

Summer watched Costa's face, the same confidence and power she'd seen yesterday radiating from him. One by one he shook hands with the old men and murmured quiet words she couldn't understand. It took him some time to restore calm, but gradually they retreated to their places in the sun.

Still the café owner stood mesmerized.

"*Endaaxi eennay, Yianni.*" Costa's tone was reassuring, as if to say everything was okay. He patted the old man on the back, and there was something touching about the way Costa smiled then, with a genuine warmth she hadn't seen the day before. Her pulse quickened at the power of it, the sincerity. She held out the coins for the coffee, but the old man batted them away.

"*Kirieh Nicoliedies, eennay!*" The café owner spoke to her, arms outspread and his bright eyes wide, as if wanting her to exclaim at the marvel of Costa standing in front of them too.

Summer nodded, impressed but slightly unnerved by the entire scene, especially her reaction to it.

"You're pretty popular." She stared intently at her cup as the waiter went back inside and Costa took the chair opposite. Again, it was his confidence that made her want to

27

shrink away. Commanding, that's what he was. Cool, in control, and commanding.

Fighting her sense of inadequacy, she lifted her chin and looked at him. He wore the dark glasses again, but today a crisp white shirt replaced the casual black T-shirt. A large and very expensive-looking watch circled his wrist. Not the watch you'd expect to see on someone desperate for a month long translating job.

"It's been a long time." He looked out toward the bay, the smile she'd seen a moment ago gone. "A long time since I've spent any time in the village. I've known most of these old men since I was a kid."

"But what a reaction," she said. "Do they behave like that for all the returned sons? It must make it hard to leave."

His chin lifted a little. "As I said, it's been a long time."

Had he enjoyed the attention or not?

Trying to avoid the subject they'd need to get to eventually, she kept things light for now. "So, Kirieh, was that a name you had as a child?"

"No." His jaw tightened, but he didn't offer an explanation. "Is Summer a nickname?"

"I wish." She chuckled. "No, it's right there on my birth certificate in indelible ink. I guess I should thank my lucky stars I wasn't named 'Moonbeam' or 'Stardust' or 'She who dances on the lily pads'."

"You don't like it?"

"Would you employ someone with a name like Summer?"

He removed his glasses but didn't answer.

The naked strength of his wordless stare made her desperate to keep talking so he couldn't sense the heat creeping down her body. "My guess is you might get past the phone call stage if you thought Summer was the worst of it, but by the time you had her whole CV and found her full name was Summer Precious Frangipani Adams...that would be that."

He rested his chin on a fist and held her gaze. "That says more about the employer than it does about her. Someone put a lot of thought into a name like that."

Was he being sarcastic? As far as she knew her mother had named her Summer because of the season she'd been conceived and the name on the incense packet by the bed.

Not so much thought.

"It just doesn't sound sincere. When I was a child, I begged Mom to change it to something traditional like...Rebecca or...Rachel. A name with integrity. Something solid."

Finally, he let out a low chuckle that set her at ease, and the tension of the morning evaporated. He nodded to the waiter as a coffee and water were placed in front of him.

"You could be like me and have the same name as practically all your male relatives." His lips quirked in a grin.

She took a sip of coffee, the sweet, nutty richness surprising. "Why's that?"

"It's Greek tradition to name the firstborn son after the paternal grandfather."

"That sounds lovely. You create a family history right there, a sense of belonging."

He shrugged powerful shoulders. "My father had five brothers whose eldest sons are all called Costa Nicoliedies and all live in this village. There's one there." He nodded to a man arranging papers at a kiosk. "There's something to be said for originality, breaking the mold."

Summer laughed before she remembered why she was here. What they had to talk about. "I guess...I just feel as though mine dates me to a time when things were more...random."

"I like it," Costa said. "It has energy."

She looked down to take another sip of coffee, her mouth suddenly dry with the intimacy of his words.

"You've decided to stay, haven't you, Summer? You've decided to agree to my...suggestion—or you wouldn't be here now. You'd be on a boat back to the mainland."

She rested the cup in its tiny saucer, fingers of fear circling her throat, afraid to look up. "I have nowhere else to turn. I need the money for this sale so I don't lose everything back home, but...it just seems so...drastic."

His silence caused her to lift her head to see his reaction.

"It would be a formality." He lowered his voice but held her gaze. "A marriage on paper. Nothing more."

Something clenched within her at his casual tone. How could someone be so blasé about something so important? And why on earth would someone go to such lengths for a complete stranger?

"I can get things arranged within two days." His stare was more intense. "Ordinarily we'd have to personally apply in Athens to get a marriage license for a foreigner, but I have a contact who can bring the paperwork straight to us. He can officiate with complete discretion and can arrange for your residency papers immediately following the proceedings."

The proceedings. Summer placed her damp palms in her lap. "I'm curious why you'd do this for someone you don't know."

He shrugged. "I'm here, you're here, there's something you need and I can help. If you stay, it means I can help you with the translation as I originally promised. And I get what I came for too. It's no more complicated than that. Take it or leave it." He pushed his chair back, and without thinking, Summer reached for him.

"Please don't go," she said. "I'm grateful. More than you can realize. But I want to know something about the man offering me his name for four weeks and how the law here will affect me. I'd be a fool if I didn't ask."

"You'll have all the privileges of a resident and the wife of a Greek citizen—everything you'll need to get the renovation done and the house sold without having to show you have money in the bank. That's all that matters. I've given up four weeks to help you achieve your goals, and this is the only way it can be done."

Something clouded his features and Summer knew it was now or never. Closing on her dream home in the States would only be possible if she sold her mother's house. If a marriage on paper, a "formality" as he put it, was the only way to achieve that, then she had to swallow any idealistic principles and just get on with it. "Okay, I'll do it," she said as her heart slammed into her throat. "I'm assuming it's easy enough to dissolve it—the m-marriage, I mean—when I leave."

He clicked his fingers. "Just like that."

Something in his tone, the emptiness in his expression, made her wonder if he knew more about temporary relationships than he was letting on.

"I must move into the house as soon as possible. I'm going to need every penny for the renovation. According to the island authorities, I need to strengthen the external walls, ensure there's adequate running water and sanitation, and whitewash the outside."

Costa leaned forward, his brow tightening and his dark eyes almost singeing her. "You can't move in. There's no furniture. And you're allergic to the dust. You could have an asthma attack all on your own. It's impossible." Again it was a statement, not a question.

"Having no furniture is nothing new for me, and I'm used to dusty places." She inched back a little. "I shared a mat on the floor with my mom for most of my childhood.

Communes aren't big on comfort. I think I have calluses in all the right places."

He shifted in his chair. "If I found you..."

He stopped mid-sentence and Summer waited.

"If you ask around the village, there's sure to be someone who'd be happy to take you in."

"I don't want to be taken in. If those communes taught me one thing, it's that the only person you can ever rely on is yourself."

She shouldn't sound ungrateful and fought to keep the bitterness from her voice, but she could think of nothing worse than being beholden to one more person. Relying on Costa for everything now, from help with the language to the entire process of renovating and selling the house, was unsettling enough. "It's almost summer. I won't freeze to death and there's an orchard behind the house where there's sure to be something to eat." She shrugged.

He looked at his watch as if to deflect his obvious shock. "That reminds me." He didn't look up. "I haven't eaten yet today, do you mind if I...?"

He couldn't have been less subtle if he tried, but Summer was thankful for his concern and something buzzed warm and low within her. "Of course not, but don't just..."

"*Yianni, rizogalo, sas parakalo,*" he called, the words flowing from his mouth like sunshine. He held up two fingers, "*Thee-o,*" and her chest lightened.

He turned back to her, his eyes warmer now, the color of melted chocolate. "Rice pudding. The best thing for breakfast."

For the first time, she realized he probably had far better things to be doing this morning than talking with her. "Since he's the mayor, what does your father think about you helping me with the house?" She wriggled in her chair as an awful thought struck. "Will you have to tell him about the...the marriage?" she whispered.

"My father has little interest in what I do now. My mother died five years ago, and as she was the connection between the two of us, we don't communicate much. I'm staying in a hotel so I don't impose."

"But if he's the mayor, surely he can find out if I have a residency permit?"

"Part of the marriage notification process in a village such as this dictates that an announcement of marriage be posted in the village square before the ceremony. He'll find out. And the rest of the village will too."

His tone hardened as he spoke about his father. What would make the words of this strong, commanding man sound so raw? His readiness to go through with the marriage simply to get around a law—for someone he hardly knew—intrigued and unsettled her.

"So what about these tradespeople?" she asked brightly, leaning back a little as Yianni placed a cornflower blue ramekin in front of her and another near Costa. "If we're going to go ahead with this, I'll need help."

"I'll speak to some people today." He picked up his spoon and plunged it into the cinnamon topping. "I'd like to have one more look around the building before they get started, though. Just to see how bad things are and how many lessons you might offer."

Summer took a bite of the pudding, its cool sweetness comforting, as she looked across at the man who would soon be her husband. Could her dream be possible after all?

CHAPTER THREE

A mind-crumbling forty-eight hours later, Summer pulled her spine straight, smoothed her pink shift dress with damp hands and concentrated on the back wall of an empty office.

No bouquet in her hand, nothing borrowed from a friend, just Costa, and making small talk like you married a stranger every day. An ancient clock, leaning at a drunken angle, ticked slowly and told her it was eight in the morning and that they'd been waiting for Costa's friend Niko for thirty minutes.

"Are you sure he'll come?"

Costa sat next to her, cool and relaxed, his ebony suit molding to his taut frame.

"I would've thought this was too early."

"Niko is doing this as a favor to me," Costa said plainly. "He flew in from Athens last night and suggested an early morning appointment before anyone else is in the office." He didn't look at her, just scanned the documents they were about to sign.

As he read the marriage license, Summer let her gaze drift through a grimy window to the view beyond. Her heart stilled. A perfect church, the purest white except for a cobalt blue dome, sat at the top of a small hill, light radiating from it and draping the surrounding trees in silver.

That's where I should be getting married.

The thought played hard and rough in her mind. Her marriage should take place in a church with a man she loved, with friends who could witness the promise she was about to make, the beautiful beginning to a future full of hope. Renovating and selling the house might fulfill one dream, but in marrying Costa this way she was shattering another.

She wrenched her gaze back. "This feels so dishonest," she said in a strangled whisper. "As if we're betraying the whole spirit of marriage. Don't you feel we're somehow cheating the government? The council?" Ourselves? Her throat grew dust-dry again, and she had to talk herself through her breathing.

His dark eyes hooked hers, and as the skin of his eyes crinkled in something like compassion, there was resignation in his steady voice. "People in my world do this all the time, Summer—to make things easier, provide a solution. It's a far better way than to marry for love only to be disappointed, to have your dreams dashed when you realize the other person doesn't feel the same way."

Although he spoke with power, something hollow sounded in his words. And that made her wonder.

"This is going to allow you to realize your dream." For the first time since they'd arrived here, his gaze really locked on hers. "It's also going to allow me to complete the job I came here to do. Neither of us has expectations of the other. I won't play games or hurt you like someone might if there were emotions involved. This is about each of us helping the other to achieve a goal, and I think that's an honorable thing to do."

She didn't want him to be honorable. As she and her mother had moved from place to place, drifting from person to person, she'd dreamed that her wedding day would be filled with passion, with quiet understanding and ecstasy. She would promise herself to a man who loved her with every part of himself, who'd give her his heart, help her build a home, and they'd start their own family. That dream had also included her mother standing by her side, giving her away with love and pride. She trapped her bottom lip between her teeth as it began to tremble.

The knowledge that would never happen, and that this moment here with Costa held none of those feelings, lay ice-heavy in her heart.

"It's not too late to pull out." His tone was more gentle. "Just say the word and we can call this off." A door banged at the front of the building and he reached for her hand, the sudden strength and warmth of it making blood rush to her cheeks. "I'm sorry for what I'm about to do," he said as he linked his fingers through hers, "but we need to make this look real, as if we just couldn't wait any longer to be together."

Summer tried to ignore the warm thread that connected his hand to her core. She tried hard to concentrate on what he was saying as the promise of his "what I'm about to do" danced lightly across her skin.

"Niko's someone I'd trust with my life, but I won't put him in a position of compromise," he said. "It won't matter so much if the villagers gossip, but Niko's job could be jeopardized if he has any hint this isn't legitimate. I've explained this needs to be secret for now, and there are reasons he accepts that, but he needs to be in no doubt this is the real thing."

Reasons he accepted his friend's marriage should be secret? What did he mean?

Footsteps echoed in the hallway outside, and Summer swallowed the disappointment that his touch wasn't genuine but pulled herself taller and gave his firm hand a squeeze. "Thank you, Costa. For doing this for me. I'll forever be grate..." As the door opened, he dragged her to him, and she had to remind herself to breathe as his lips covered hers. Shock and excitement and unchecked desire rocketed through her as time stopped.

Her whole body melted under Costa's touch. Her hands twined around his neck and she pulled him closer, deepening the kiss that should have been all about show and pretense, but was a treasure, a gift. The essence of him that had before now been elusive and secret now filled her senses in every way possible.

His lips were soft and warm; his tongue gently stroked the edge of her mouth as she inhaled the heady, male scent of him. He cupped her face in his hands as if she were the most precious thing in the world, and she hoped he didn't notice the swift and strong pulse that was beating through her blood.

Gently, he pulled away and, gazing deep into her eyes, gave her the warmest, most toe-curling smile she'd ever seen, his eyes dancing.

How could something so false make her body burn and bend like molten glass? Over and over she told herself this wasn't real, but if it was all a lie, why was every nerve ending in her traitorous body aching to be close to him again?

When he moved his gaze from her to Niko and then reached down to squeeze her hand, she realized the feeling wasn't stopping, no matter how much she wished it would.

And a thought struck her between the eyes.

How could she spend all her time here with this man—a

man who saw her as a business transaction—when her body reacted to him like this? She'd never survive an entire month.

~

"What can you see? Is it dark? What if it's a nest of snakes?" Summer held tight to the bottom of the old wooden ladder and tried not to look at the calves directly in front of her. Calves that appeared to have been hewn from virgin granite. The calves of the man who'd been her husband for all of two hours.

The thought that she was now married, a wife, was just as surreal now as it was when they'd signed the papers. She looked down at the gold ring he'd placed on her finger only a short time ago and sighed. If she was going to concentrate on the really hard work of renovating, she'd have to forget she was a wife, ignore the warm little thrill every time she thought of being married to a man who moved and intrigued her more than she wanted to admit.

When they'd returned to the house and changed into shorts and T-shirts, Costa had insisted he inspect the rest of the rooms so he could organize tradespeople straight away. She'd shown him into another room with a hole in one wall and then down to the basement, which was in pretty good condition. Now he was up the ladder searching for the source of the scrabbling noise.

"It's definitely a nest." His voice was muffled. "But it's not snakes."

A scraping sound indicated something being dragged across the ceiling, before he started climbing down. Corded muscles flexed in his tanned calves. With effort, she lifted her gaze to see that he carried a wooden box and had to balance it on each of the rungs as he made his way down.

"It's nesting in there!" She jumped back, and the ladder wobbled. "What is it?"

"*Helithonya*," he said as his foot reached the floor. "You have swallows nesting in your roof. It'll be easy enough to block the holes so they can't get back in again, but it'll be better to do that from the outside. Looks like they've been having plenty of fun up there." He placed the box on the floor. "And I found this."

A tiny dart stabbed her heart, throbbing for a second before slowly fading. It had been her mother's. She could tell the moment she stepped closer.

The box was scratched and worn, and a faded label on the side displayed the name Caroline Adams.

She looked at Costa and fought the tremble in her voice. "It was my mom's."

She blew her fringe away; suddenly it was hot in here. "It's so weird that I knew nothing about this part of her life. Well, not until I read her will. This house must've been the most substantial thing she ever owned, but she never told me about it. Not even when..." She stopped herself telling the whole, heartbreaking story of the last few months. He didn't need to know about it, and if she thought too hard, she'd finish in a curled-up ball, crying in the corner. "I wonder why she bought it. It doesn't fit with how she just moved from place to place with me."

She walked to the window, away from the box and the secrets it might hold. "I knew she'd traveled and taught here and there, but when she talked about it, every place seemed to blend into the other. Turkey, Morocco, Tunisia—I guess she must have been looking for somewhere better, somewhere she could find happiness. She kept on traveling even when she got home, one way or another."

Looking back, she found Costa watching her. "I'm sorry," he said, his tone gentle. "If you'd rather I put it back, take it away...I just thought there was no point leaving it up there where it might never be found."

"It's fine. Can't imagine there's much in it. I mean, as far as I know, Mom never intended to come back here, so why would she have left anything important behind?"

A sense of emptiness and confusion pushed into her heart —the same feelings she'd had when she'd stumbled across the bead. The thought of finding pieces of her mother throughout the house suddenly made her panic. Things were too raw, her emotions still locked down too tight.

"Would you mind just putting it over there in the corner? I'll clean it out sometime."

Costa wasn't sure how much longer he could keep up this charade. It would only be a matter of time before Summer put two and two together and realized he would've been on the island when her mother lived here. That part didn't really matter. It was the promise he'd made to Caroline that had to stay secret. And now he and Summer were married, that promise felt heavier. The sooner they could get this job done, the better.

She stood at the window, her slim shoulders hunched in a white singlet. He was no counselor, but clearly this mother/daughter relationship hadn't been an easy one. His own relationship with his dad was difficult. Maybe he and Summer had more in common than he'd first thought.

Caroline had said in one of their last phone calls that she couldn't bear to think of Summer doing all this on her own. He just needed to be there. Well, actually, she hadn't even asked him to do that. She'd only wanted him to make sure her daughter could sell the house and return safely to the States.

Caroline knew he'd hardly been home the last ten years—and all she'd said was that she knew he'd help. Not even she could've imagined the lengths he'd need to go to fulfill his promise. But he'd do it. Marrying Summer this morning might not have been honoring the laws of this island, but he'd had to go through with it to honor Caroline—the woman who'd given him a sense of who he could truly be. She was the only adult in his life who'd believed he could end up where he was today—successful, wealthy, and confident in who he was.

"So when do we start?" The smile on Summer's face was a practiced one, tight and emotionless. For the first time, he realized what a huge ask this must be for her. She looked so vulnerable and scared beneath her tough veneer. This must be an overwhelming experience. It didn't seem right that her first time away from the States was such a negative one. He was used to traveling all over the world, dealing with different people. She wasn't.

"I've talked to three people." He moved the box to the corner of the room, then sat down beside it, glad they could finally make some plans for how they'd tackle this house. "Takis is a plumber and also one of my cousins."

"Not Costa?"

Her smile warmed a little and something sparked in him, a desire to see her do it again. "Actually, yes, but as he's the shortest of all the Costas, we call him Costakis, 'little Costa,' and Takis for short."

Now there was a genuine smile. It lit her entire face and her beautiful blue eyes seemed bigger, brighter on her delicate features. "Oh, that's lovely!" Her laugh took flight, filled the whole room with a sense of life that made him take note to try to make it happen more often.

"Takis will come and look at the plumbing soon. He doesn't need lessons himself, but his daughter has school exams in a few weeks. She needs a good mark in English to be accepted into a London fashion school. He said he'd be happy to trade work for lessons."

Shoulders relaxing, Summer sat on the floor in front of him, her slim legs crossed at the ankles.

"Socrates, the plasterer, will come tomorrow morning."

"You're joking?" she said, wide-eyed.

"Sorry?"

"Someone called Socrates will do my plastering?" The laugh again.

"Ah, right. Socrates is a common name on the island too. You'll probably also meet the odd Achilles, and Mr. Plato owns the bookshop."

Her head shook, her eyes bright with wonder. "What will they think of me though? How will we do all this when I don't speak any Greek? I can see how I'll communicate with Takis' daughter, but what about Socrates and Takis? How could it work?"

"Socrates sings in one of the nightclubs. He doesn't speak much English, but he needs help with the pronunciation of English song lyrics for a competition that's coming up." Costa rubbed his chin. He'd chosen Socrates and Takis knowing they wouldn't know or care about Summer's mother or what he was doing for her. But to ensure everything went the way Caroline had wanted, he'd have to be with Summer as often as he could. "Also, I'll be here to help with Takis."

"What do you mean?" Her voice had softened and the panicked look she'd carried in her eyes yesterday wasn't so pronounced.

"You need someone to read the council specifications for you, and you can't spend your entire day giving English lessons. I'll do whatever building work needs doing, and it'll mean I can be here to help while you're teaching."

Silence pulsed between them.

"There's something wrong?" Was she angry with his interference? Things had been going well. Tension ratcheted his spine. "This will be the best way."

Then he saw the tears. As they welled, her chin trembled, and he fought the sudden, overwhelming urge to be close to her. To hold and comfort her.

"Thank you so much." She stood and turned away, but he caught the wobble of her chin and read her body language that screamed to stay away. "I really appreciate all this, Costa." She moved to the ladder and carried it away from the ceiling. "Everything you're doing for me."

He clenched and unclenched his fists, hoping physical movement might halt the back and forth in his brain.

Summer deserved to know the truth about why he was doing this, but he'd promised. A last promise to a dying woman wasn't easily broken, especially when that woman was responsible for everything that defined you.

His fingers balled into fists once more. No. He couldn't let Summer think this was all some convenient coincidence —that he'd married her out of the goodness of his heart. If he waited and she found out later, it might destroy her memories of her mother forever. He had to tell her everything.

"Summer, there's something you should know."

She turned, concerned at the tone of his voice, worried her tears might've changed his mind. What was wrong with her lately? Two months since her mom had died, and any tiny thing could still send the familiar clutch to her throat and sting to her eyes.

A change in his look, an intensity she hadn't seen before

and an intimacy as if he'd guessed something, quickened the words from her mouth.

"I'll pay you well." She spoke firmly, attempting to stem the inevitable, her fingers closing around the frigid tiki at her neck. "You can't be expected to do all this for nothing. I can't give you anything now, but as soon as I sell the house you'll get everything owed to you."

Oh, please, God, don't let him back out now, not after the lengths I've gone through to get this done; I can't do any of this without him.

She needed to harness his charisma, the strange magnetism he seemed to possess for the people of the village.

He began to speak, but she cut him off. "I don't like to be in anyone's debt, and if I had a choice, I wouldn't be here trying to do all this. I'll completely understand if you want to..." Her hands shook and her cheeks burned.

He stood, pulling himself to his full height and towering above her. She willed with all her might that this time he'd be on her side. "Takis will be here soon and I need to explain—"

The knock on the door cut his words short and a chasm of silence fell between them. His expression transformed into one of frustration.

Another knock and Summer held her breath, silently commanding him not to leave her alone.

"Takis? *Essee eenay?*" Costa called, his stare holding Summer still. The rich guttural sound of his words sent a delicious shiver up her spine.

Finally, he looked away as the noise of someone repeat-edly trying the latch became louder.

"Can you explain?" she asked Costa, hoping she was hiding her relief that his chance to back out had passed. "He must come through the window."

Costa spoke again, but this time louder, a rich river of

sound as individual words became indefinable, each running into the next.

A beaming face with the same striking features as Costa, but on a much smaller frame, appeared at the window.

"*Kalimera!*" the man called brightly, tipping the black felt hat on his head.

It didn't take long for Costa to introduce Summer and explain things to Takis—well, she presumed that's what he was doing and hoped he wasn't mentioning anything about the marriage.

All the while, Takis stood outside the window, nodding, his relaxed features proving they were discussing nothing more than plumbing and building. Eventually, Costa grabbed hold of his cousin's arm to heave him through.

"I'll show him around." Costa's English broke the dreamy spell his native tongue had cast over her and Summer blinked, forcing herself to concentrate as he continued. "So he can see the extent of the work to be done. He doesn't speak much English, but he says his daughter Athina will come and find you tomorrow for a lesson, if that's okay."

Summer nodded.

He showed Takis through to the bathroom, then turned back to her. "We'll have a quick look at the water heater and see if we can get it going. If we're going to move in here, it must work."

Breath rushed from her lungs. "What do you mean, *we* move in? We didn't discuss...that's not part—"

"If you want to ensure you're not investigated by immigration, then I must move in," he whispered. "And besides, I don't want to arrive here one morning to find you unconscious from an asthma attack."

"I've told you," Summer began, as every reason this was a terrible idea raced through her mind, "I'm already too much in your debt as it is. And what will your friends and family think?" What else could she say? The thought of waking up in the same house as him every morning filled her with dread and...anticipation.

"They'll think we're married, of course. We can't risk anyone finding out our relationship isn't real or you won't be able to see the house sale through. I'll have a double bed delivered tomorrow. You'll have to keep it in here until we fix up the hole in the bedroom."

"And people won't think it strange? You secretly marrying someone they've never seen before."

"Trust me." His features hardened. "People will be more than ready to believe it."

What on earth did that mean? She covered her face in desperation.

"It'll be fine, Summer. If you want this to work, then this is the way it has to be."

She took a lungful of air, her hand still over her face.

"And if you want to stop worrying Takis as we go through the house," Costa said more gently, "try to look a little less horrified."

She forced a smile at Costa's cousin as they moved through to the bathroom, but she couldn't stop her thoughts racing. How could she manage it? She thought she'd agreed to the worst of it. Now this?

"If you're okay, I'll show Takis around the rest of the house," Costa said.

She drew in a shaky breath and gave him a quick nod. She had to start acting like this was all very simple, that she had the confidence to pull it off. If only she truly felt that way.

Costa and Takis moved off, with the shorter man whistling through his teeth every time they made a closer inspection of something and causing Summer to wince. Every exclamation probably meant she needed a lot more money.

When they moved through to the next room, she decided not to follow. The bad news would come her way soon enough and then she'd have to work out if she was going to stay here. If *they* were going to stay here.

The thought of him being here every day, every night, didn't get any easier, but she had to admit that only Costa's continued presence was preventing a full-blown panic attack. His calm, reasoned advice was one of the few things stopping her from running away. And if she were honest, she hadn't been looking forward to living in this tumbledown house alone and unable to speak the language.

She turned, and the dark wooden box in the corner of the room caught her eye. Her stomach looped, and she knew she had to open it. The very existence of this house was unbelievable enough, but she couldn't understand why her mother would leave a box of her things here—unless she'd meant to return.

That hardly seemed likely. Her mom never had enough money to travel outside the States, except for one trip to New Zealand after she'd trained as a midwife.

Bending, she pushed it to a spot in the middle of the room where a shaft of light illuminated the packed earth floor. Curiosity and sick trepidation burned deep as she brushed dust from the top, carefully undid the weatherbeaten latch at the front and lifted the creaking lid.

She whooshed out a breath. As she'd expected, there was very little inside. Her mother had always scoffed at "material possessions," condemned them as "symbols of greed" and "plugs to fill empty souls". All of which made the existence of the box even more unusual.

Lifting a purple scarf, she found beads, a couple of books about the Greek Islands, a collection of shells, and at the bottom, a photograph and a ragged piece of turquoise fabric that had been folded into a small parcel.

She picked up the fabric and carefully unwrapped it, the material soft against her searching fingers. Inside was a ring —a simple gold band. A family heirloom, perhaps? She'd never known her mother to keep jewelry of any monetary value.

It looked like a wedding band, but given her mother's cynicism about marriage, Summer suspected it would be more likely to be a charm to symbolize her "marriage" to the universe, or something equally Zen. When she held it up to the sunlight, she could see Greek script written inside the band—με όλη μου την αγάπη. Πάντα. Had her mother found it? Bought it herself? If someone had given it to her, surely she would've taken it with her.

As the ring warmed in her hand, the briefest touch of emotion brushed her heart as she thought of her marriage to Costa. What would it be like to have someone like him place a gold ringer on her finger out of love, rather than obligation or convenience?

As quickly as the thought had come, she pushed it aside. These treacherous feelings and regrets couldn't keep creeping up on her like this. She'd sell the ring and use the money for the renovations. If it'd had any real significance for her mom, she wouldn't have left it here, forgotten in a ceiling cavity thousands of miles away.

Quickly, she wrapped it in its cloth and put it back in the box. It would be safe there, at least until she found someone to tell her if it was genuine.

"What have you found?" Costa leaned against the door-jamb, watching her, and Summer was glad she'd hidden the ring. The less he knew about her real feelings concerning marriage—that it should be the cornerstone of the deepest love—and the way her mother had avoided it, the better.

"Oh, just odds and ends." She kept her voice light as she

reached into the box one more time and pulled out the photograph.

"Your mother's things?" He took a step into the room, but she couldn't look at him. Her gaze was glued to the snapshot, goosebumps dancing on her skin. It was a small black and white print with a white border. The surface was covered with fine scratches, as if it had been handled many times. Caught at the edge of the photo was her mother and a man—obviously Greek—looking into each other's eyes with the private intensity exclusive to new-bloomed lovers.

If it had been a photograph of anyone else, Summer wouldn't have bitten down on her bottom lip, and the all too familiar drag of disappointment might not have pulled at her heart.

"Just a holiday snap," she said breezily. "Nothing valuable." But the leaden weight of her mom's life and death sat solid in her heart. How long had this love affair lasted? More than the two weeks her mother had had with her father when she'd returned to the States? The only things to have come out of that relationship were Summer and an awful lot of antagonism.

"A photograph of her?" Costa took another step closer.

Turning the photograph over, she read to herself, "Agios Georgios beach—M and Me, August."

Who were you? Why didn't you let me in to this part of your life? Maybe I would've understood.

Sad, tearful voices whispered in Summer's ear and she placed the photograph on the lid of the box. "Just a picture from a long, long time ago. Nothing important."

What had she expected to find? A detailed exposé on what had led her mom to be so carefree her entire life? Had she expected to find the key that might unlock the part of her mother's heart where all thought of commitment and responsibility might have lain?

She looked up at Costa, then back to the photo. While she couldn't change the past, she was completely clear on what she wanted for her future—she would never let that sort of part-time love slither its way into her life. Not now. Not ever.

CHAPTER FOUR

*C*osta ripped a hunk of bread from the corner of a crusty brown loaf, and Summer watched the flex of a bicep as he reached to hand it to her. After Takis had left, Costa had gone into the village and returned with bread, cheese and fat black olives. Now they sat in the sun at the back of the house, looking out across the orange grove. The smell of over-ripe oranges wafted past periodically on a warming breeze.

A lot of work needed to be done this afternoon if she—her heart swooped again as she corrected herself—if *they* were going to move in tomorrow, but Costa had insisted she eat first. She had questions she wanted to ask him, anyway.

The midday sun warmed the wall of the house behind her back. Pushing a little harder into it, she marveled that this was all hers, every last stone, every chipped piece of plaster.

"Takis thinks he can be finished in two weeks." Costa unwrapped the cheese from waxy white paper. "He always exaggerates, though, so I don't think the job's as bad as he tried to make out."

Summer, unable to reply as she chewed the deliciously sour crust, waved for him to continue.

"Once he's checked all the plumbing, made sure everything's watertight and replaced a few pipes, then we can start with the building."

He pulled a red Swiss army knife from his back pocket, flicked it open and stabbed a hunk of cheese, then passed it to her on the end of the blade.

Such a primitive act that caused a primitive thrill inside her.

She concentrated harder on the point of the knife, grateful for an excuse not to look him directly in the eye in case he could sense that thrill.

"I'll fix the front door," he said, still watching her, his gaze drawing her in. "If we're going to move in here tomorrow, we can't be leaping through the window."

She stopped chewing. "About that. Is it necessary? Won't it just cause problems for you—staying here with me?"

"It'll cause far bigger problems if I don't and immigration investigates." He rubbed a hand across his stubbled chin. "I always stay in a hotel when I'm back here anyway." He paused, and when she looked up, a muscle moved at his jaw. "My father and I have trouble being under the same roof so it won't bother him. No one else needs to know any more about why I'm living here. As far as they're concerned, I'll be working here from early morning until late at night. Unless you're not comfortable with it?"

Her cheeks heated as she looked down and crumbled a piece of bread in her fingers. "I'm still struggling to get my head around being married to you, let alone thinking about you moving in."

"You had no other option."

"I know." She made a circle with the crumbs. "It's just not what I'd planned." Changing the subject would keep things practical and away from the personal. "Did Takis mention what sort of price I might get for the house?"

Costa tensed, and she looked up.

"What?"

"Wouldn't it be nice to keep it?" he asked quietly, rubbing his palms across his shorts, his gaze roaming her face. "We could still renovate so it would be a place to come back to, a place to remember your mother. By the time you pay taxes and do exchange rates, will it really be worth it to sell?"

She swallowed, and the cheese stung the back of her throat. "Yes." She tried to keep the emotion from her voice, but it cracked a little. "Yes, I think it will be worth selling this so I can finally have something to call my own, in a place I choose to live, with things I choose to have around me. Besides, I have friends and a life back home."

Her best friend Chloe had called last night and asked her the same question. "Forget the house in Brentwood Bay," she'd said. "Take some time and spread your wings. Don't rush to get tied down with a mortgage." But Chloe still had Sunday lunches with her parents in the house she'd grown up in. Still drove her grandma every Sunday to the church where she and her three brothers had been christened. Chole would never know the gnawing desire to be stable and secure that still ran deep through Summer.

"It's such a shame, though." He shrugged and broke off a piece of bread for himself before offering her more. "Such a traditional house, so unspoiled by things modern."

If he was so interested in maintaining old houses, why wasn't he living in the village? "By the looks of it, no one's lived here for a long time."

"Wouldn't you like to think a house that had been your mother's for thirty years could stay in the family?"

Family. He didn't know the effect that word had on her.

How could he? She answered as calmly as she was able. "I have no family."

He looked startled for a second, then recovered himself.

"Do you have a house in the village?" she asked, curious to know more about him.

"Only my father's house."

For a moment there was silence, Summer hoping she'd made her point.

He looked thoughtful as he chewed the bread, so she continued. "I doubt I'd ever come back here. My mom never spoke much about being in Greece, so the house can't have been that important to her. She never placed much value in material things."

Costa swallowed. "In what way?"

Summer reached for an olive. She wouldn't normally feel comfortable speaking about her life with someone she hardly knew, but something about the view and the tangle of feelings coiling inside her made her want to justify her beliefs, to explain to this man—her husband—why she had to sell the house.

"We lived in communes." She drew her knees up to her chest. "With lots of people. Couples, children, single people and solo mothers with children like Mom and me."

"You had brothers and sisters?"

"We *called* everyone brother and sister, but I never had a real one." She crossed her ankles, breathed in, then let out a ragged sigh. "I was the result of a brief relationship and my mom said she never wanted more children of her own."

"Was her death sudden?"

The raw, honest nature of his question caused her to swing her head away. As always when she thought about her mom's death two months ago, she focused on something distant. She could pretend she was talking about someone else as her throat burned.

Two swallows were pulling pieces of dry grass from around the base of an orange tree. Her eyes remained fixed on them, the rhythmic nature of their task soothing her.

"Her death was more sudden than it needed to be, but it wasn't a shock, no."

Even though her eyes remained straight ahead, she could feel his stare. "She wouldn't talk about it. Just kept on being positive, as she'd always done. She refused to discuss funerals, that sort of thing."

One swallow, a bundle of grass in its beak, flew toward the house, straight above her head. She lifted her face to watch it dip under the eaves and disappear.

"Oh, no!" She jumped up. "Did you see that?" The smooth thrim, thrim beat above her head showed the second swallow had followed the first. "We're too late now!"

"Too late for what?" Costa stood, his gaze trained on the side of the house.

"We can't possibly plug the hole now. They're building a nest!"

Summer stood, hands on hips, earnestly waiting for the swallows to reappear.

This woman was one big contradiction.

She'd never traveled outside her own country, but now she was prepared to live in a house for a month without running water or electricity. One second she talked about having to return to her job and mortgage, and the next she spoke about growing up in communes. Not to mention her beliefs about marriage and what they'd just done.

His gaze followed her as she moved closer to the house. Sometimes she seemed delicate and fragile, but other times, especially when she spoke her mind, there was a strength to her that was powerfully attractive.

He was quite sure she had no idea how stunning she was, or how mesmerizing. Often, she'd speak with her head tilted slightly down, her blonde fringe a small curtain for her to hide behind. Although she wore a singlet that accentuated the full curve of her breasts, more often than not she had her arms crossed—a first line of defense he wanted to break through.

And now the swallows. If she wanted to renovate this house properly, she couldn't be put off by a few birds.

"They'll make a mess." He followed her to stand under the eaves. "Bits of straw and mud everywhere. Bird poop. Not such an attractive proposition for a potential buyer."

"But they mate for life!" she exclaimed, turning to glare at him as if he'd suggested roasting them alive. Her lips, normally slightly apart, pursed in an angry little pout. Frighteningly kissable.

"What if they've lived here for years?" She flicked her fringe back for a change. "Or been parents to hundreds of swallowlings or whatever they're called? I can't just take that away from them." Her indignation was becoming such an unexpected turn on, the most sensible response now was silence.

"Perhaps we could build a little box up there—with its own floor so you couldn't hear them from below. That might work, right?"

He didn't have to answer as the swallows reappearing diverted her attention. They flew back down to the orange tree and began pulling at the dry grass again.

"Is this all your mother's land?" Costa asked, trying to distance his thoughts from the curve of her body, the set of her lips, and what she'd just said about mating for life.

What was it about her that made him want to ease the

pain of all this for her? The more time he spent with her, the deeper his need get closer, to touch, but something made him want even more than that.

He followed her to stand closer to the swallows. He had to tell her. He couldn't go on pretending their link was some random event. This lack of control, the restrictions on what he could and couldn't say to her, were pushing him to a limit he thought he'd never have to reach again.

Now was the time. He had to tell her something so she wouldn't despise him completely if she found out the whole truth about her mother asking him to look out for her.

"I think it's all her land." She held a hand above her eyes to block the sun, the first line of defense gone, the full form of her body beautifully revealed. "I might need you to help me read the deed, though. I think she lived here with quite a few people, so maybe one of them owns it."

"I don't think she lived with lots of people."

Summer slowly turned to face him, her porcelain cheeks turning alabaster white. Her slow breaths in and quick breaths out signaled that she'd made the connection, and he clenched a fist at the sudden knowledge he'd hurt her.

"You knew her, didn't you?"

He hesitated. He had to be so careful—giving away enough information to maintain his integrity while holding back what was necessary to keep his promise wouldn't be easy. "I was a kid," he said simply, holding her widening gaze. "She was a teacher at the local school."

"I suppose she'd be hard to forget with her long skirts and bare feet."

She smiled, but Costa sensed hurt in her voice. Why would a daughter who'd spent so much time with her mother have such conflicted feelings about her?

"I don't think she was that unusual." He watched her, trying to work out how the conversation would progress, how he might end it and steer clear of questions he couldn't answer. "There were quite a few itinerants in the village then, people from all over the world looking for an idyllic lifestyle. She just fitted in with them."

Summer scoffed, turning away and crouching in the dust, pulling at pieces of dried grass. "I don't understand any of it," she said without looking at him. "Why would she keep this house, decades after leaving here? If she'd sold it all those years ago, we might have had something in our lives. We might not have had to scrounge and beg and rely on other people. If we'd had enough money, I might've been able to..." She let out a sigh and turned back to Costa, the look on her face sending primal instincts rushing through him. He wanted to protect her, provide for her, give her a history she could be proud of.

Then her gaze strengthened. "If she'd sold this, I might have had a real home."

Later that afternoon, Summer dragged her dilapidated suitcase up to the window at the front of the house. How on earth could she hoist her case through?

The pension owner had loaded her bags on the back of a sweet little donkey and Summer had followed the man and his beast down the narrow, cobbled hill, every few steps a giggle sneaking up on her at the image. The donkey and his owner clip-clopped back up the lane now as the man waved back and called, "*Yah-sas.*"

Costa had said he wanted to help her move in tomorrow, but she'd decided that saving one night's accommodation meant more cash in the renovation coffers. And besides, she was a little uncomfortable about everything Costa was doing for her. If she could get in and settled before he moved in, she'd feel more in control. She'd read enough self-help books to know her need for control came from having very little growing up. It was both a blessing and a curse.

Something niggled at the back of her mind. His story about being home for the summer, and the apparent ease with which he'd suggested marriage, didn't quite make sense. He'd said he hadn't been back to the island much in the last few years, and yet he hadn't spoken of doing anything while he was here—except to help her. And the expensive-looking watch hinted at more than a career as a translator. Over lunch, he'd mentioned his plans for the renovation, what each of them would need to do. It all went far beyond a simple translation job.

She tugged on the suitcase, ready to go around the back of the building where she now knew there was another door, when a rattle from inside turned her blood to ice.

"Costa?" she called hopefully, an image of a hissing pit of snakes, or perhaps something slimy and four-legged, making her stumble back.

More rattling, and then suddenly the big wooden door scraped back and there he was. Shirtless.

"Oh…I…What?" Words wouldn't form themselves into intelligent sentences. No matter how hard she willed her brain to connect with the muscles in her jaw, she couldn't form a logical thought, let alone say it. Her pulse played a tattoo at her throat as she surveyed the length of him.

She'd seen abdomens like this before, on late night TV infomercials for the latest whizz-bang exercise equipment, but they'd always been headless, shiny things that looked more at home in an abattoir than on a man. This one was lean and glowing like a polished chestnut. Momentarily, her gaze swung to the line of ebony hair below his navel, and as her thoughts caught up to what she was seeing, she swallowed and forced her gaze upward.

Such a different view to the previous way she'd seen him, business-like, professional. Covered.

"Summer. I'm sorry." No smile, and no sense of embarrassment either. The only person heating here was her, from her cheeks downward. "I had to remove the door, take it off its hinges to straighten the line," he said, as if in explanation for his state of undress. "It took a bit of time to put it back together again."

He slowly reached behind and pulled a T-shirt from the back of his jeans, before dragging it, towel-like, across the top of his chest. It looked brand new, pristine white, and she now imagined his scent imprinted on it forever—a fresh, woodsy scent that made her a little dizzy.

"I didn't realize you'd come back this afternoon." He dragged an arm across his forehead causing that abdomen to pull taut, hard, and she swallowed heavily. "I wanted to have this working when you moved in." His gaze shifted from her face to the suitcase and he frowned. "Are you doing that now?"

She turned to look at her luggage too. It gave her an excuse to steady her breathing and pull herself together.

"I thought I would." She bent to take hold of a handle. "No point leaving a perfectly good house uninhabited, and besides, I'm saving every penny I have for the reno." Pulling the suitcase behind her and head down, she made her way through the door, acutely aware of Costa now pulling the T-shirt over his head.

"Is this all you have?" he asked, the rest of her bags now resting easily in his arms. "How will you cook? Eat? What will you—?"

"You don't need to worry, Costa." The muscles in her back tightened as she pulled herself straighter. "You've gone way beyond your job description as it is. As I told you this morning, I'm quite used to living without luxuries." She turned to him and smiled, forcing her gaze to meet his, even though she knew it would increase the warmth in her cheeks. His brow lowered and he crossed his arms over his chest.

"The woman at the pensione insisted she'd bring dinner down for me tonight and her husband will set up a small gas stove. I have a bedroll and a blanket in my suit..."

Her breath hitched in her throat as something caught her eye, and she stopped and stared. A double bed was nestled in the corner of the room. A bed with pillows and blankets and a comforter that looked like it was made for arctic conditions.

"Where on earth...?" She moved to it, then stroked the crisp cotton of a pillowslip. She sat down on the cloud-like comforter and turned to Costa. "Did you do this?"

He turned away as if to continue with the door. "I helped Yiannis from the café bring it in." He knelt on the ground with a hammer and what looked like part of a bolt. "You couldn't stay here without a bed."

"The linen, the blankets...?"

"From the village," he said, as if that really told her anything. What she really wanted to know was who'd bought them. "I'm not answering any more questions," he said, his tone gruff. "I need to get this latch finished before dark."

The hammer came down hard on the bolt and the ring of metal on metal echoed about the room. "I suggest you get the fire started so you'll at least have some hot water to wash with in the morning. I wasn't planning on moving in until late tomorrow."

"It's fixed?"

She waited while he hit the bolt again.

"Takis checked the firebox and all the pipework. He said it's fine to use." He didn't turn around but raised the hammer over his head once more and struck the piece of iron. The T-shirt might mask his torso, but her eyes were drawn to his flexing muscles.

She couldn't make him out. Was he annoyed with her? Angry? As she moved through to the bathroom, something else caught her eye. Inside a stunning turquoise bowl, oranges were piled high. Where had they come from? Had he picked them?

"Your neighbor said it was wrong that you had a whole orange grove but no bowl to put them in," he said from the other room, as if reading her mind.

The man from the *kafenion*, a shop owner, the neighbor—she didn't know these people. Why would they want to do things like this? Nobody had owned anything outright in the commune, and she'd always assumed that in the wider world people would be less generous, more suspicious. Something touched her deeply then, as she thought about how impossible this all would have been on her own.

The door of the firebox was open, with the makings of a fire inside. A box of matches sat on the hearth.

He hadn't come back here on the off chance to fix the door. Costa must have been here for most of the afternoon, helping with the bed, laying the fire like this. The tight cord of emotion that always sat just outside her thoughts shifted a little. She gathered it up, pushing her feelings further away, determined not to let it unravel—that control habit again. There was a job to be done here. That was all.

Just a job to be done.

She struck a match and held it against the paper in the grate. The dry twigs on top immediately caught alight and crackled to life.

Leaving the door of the fire open, she walked over to the window. The sun was setting, the sky beyond the hills fading from peach to gold. A warm breeze carried the hollow call of a dove and she smiled at the thought of the swallows in her ceiling, building their own little home. It was right that they shouldn't be moved.

"Light. You don't have any light." Turning, she saw Costa standing in the doorway, the top of his head brushing the lintel. The powerful features, the intense look; she still couldn't read him, but she was a little over his concern, which bordered on patronizing. She might be his wife, but she could look after herself the same way she had before she'd met him.

"I have the light on my phone." She turned back to the window. He really thought she wasn't capable of looking after herself. "I'll be fine. There'll be light from the fire for a while and then I can go to sleep."

"The lock's working now. If you're frightened at all..."

"Just stop, please!" The force behind her words took her by surprise. But something had snapped inside.

He might be the most breathtaking specimen of manhood she'd ever laid eyes on, and he'd helped her out of a sticky spot, but she was used to taking care of herself.

His eyes widened. A slight lift in his eyebrows dared her to go further, to tell him what she really thought. He took a step into the room.

Leaning against the wall, she looked him square in the eye. "Look, I'm incredibly grateful for everything you've done. You've gone way beyond what I'd hoped for, but I'm fine now. I don't want you to think you need to protect me. I'm capable of looking after myself."

Waiting for him to speak was unsettling; he just stared, his ebony gaze fixed firmly on her.

"It's just...I'm not used to having other people do things for me and...it makes me uncomfortable. I don't enjoy feeling I might owe you something."

"You owe me nothing." He stayed still, the words spoken

so quietly she might have missed them but for his firm tone stressing their importance.

"If only I had money," she said. "If only I'd had the fifty thousand, I wouldn't have needed to bother you with all this. I'd have been able to do justice to the renovation, had enough to get this house up to scratch before I sell it. If I had money, I could..."

"What?" He thrust his hands deep in his pockets, the strength of his tone intensifying. "If you had money, you might never have come here, might never have seen where your mother lived or experienced some of the things she did. What would you do with money here? Tell me. I'm interested."

She pulled her gaze from his and looked around the room, glad of a chance to hide her real feelings. "Carpets. I'd buy carpets." She waved her hands in emphasis. "As a teenager I'd visit my school friends and just stand in their lounge rooms, barefoot, so I could feel the warmth beneath my feet. You put carpets in a house because you know you're never going to leave. I hate bare boards and bare floors." She scuffed the packed earth beneath her sandals. "I'd put carpets down so I'd know I belonged here."

"What else?"

"Ornaments."

"Ornaments? What do you mean?"

She paced in front of the window. "Things. Just things I'd bought because they reminded me of a holiday, or a boyfriend, or a long-lost aunt. I'd have them all over the house so I could look at them whenever I wanted." Her words quickened. "They might make me mad or sad; they might be the ugliest thing anyone had ever given me, but they'd be mine and they'd stay in the same place. And so would I."

He moved to tend the fire, and it was then she noticed the

detail of his boots—rich brown leather with two initials stamped on a tag at the side. Of course, she'd never been within a thousand miles of the Italian designer, but the mark was unmistakable.

"Why are you doing all this for me?" she asked. The watch. The boots. The reactions of the villagers to him—had she missed something? "Marrying me, buying furniture and linen, organizing the renovation of this house. I can tell you probably have much more important things to do with your summer than charity work."

He spun around, halting her words. "I have bought nothing." His eyes glinted. "And by your attitude, I can see you're far from being a charity case." He took a breath and slowly turned back to the fire. "People in this village are very caring," he finally said. "They are not so driven by money that they're selfish or greedy. They like to help each other."

She realized how ungrateful she'd sounded, and shame swept through her. "I'm sorry." She walked away from the window, where the breeze had become chill. "I'm just not used to having people do things for me." She sat down on the floor, a few feet from him. "Part of the lifestyle my mother lived involved me being encouraged to think as an individual from a very young age, not relying on others to make my decisions for me."

"There's nothing weak about listening to, and sometimes even taking direction from, others." He put a larger piece of wood on the fire and closed the door. Drawing himself back to his full height, he brushed his hands on his jeans. "If you'd rather do all of this yourself now we've got around the legal side, you only need to say the word."

It had come out all wrong. Her frustration, the magnitude of this task and, if she were honest with herself, Costa's very physical presence had all put her on the defensive. She desperately needed his help if she was going to get this house finished, so perhaps the best thing would be if she kept her emotions to herself.

"I'm really sorry. What I said came out all wrong." She stood up, a painful lump forming in her throat. It looked as though he might leave, and that terrified her. "I don't know whether it's the shock of the marriage, the jet lag, or the nerves at what I'm about to undertake, but I shouldn't have become so upset and defensive. If you'd really known my mother, you'd understand how she would've loved this whole scenario, me trying to 'climb the mountain of my soul' as she used to put it. I'm sure after a good sleep I'll be less cranky and ready to get into some hard work."

Costa rubbed a hand across a jaw she would swear grew darker by the minute, nodded, then walked straight out the door.

CHAPTER FIVE

*C*osta had thought twice about bringing Summer breakfast. It was clear she was insanely independent and reluctant to accept help, but she'd be no good today if she didn't eat. His aunts and neighbors had been dropping food off at his hotel since he'd arrived and he was glad he could share it with her.

And there was something else. He wanted her to accept his help. Ever since she'd first spoken, he could see how closed off she was, suspicious even. He wanted her to unfold, to soften and bloom, allowing him to then peel back the layers and find the essence of this woman.

He balanced the box of food and crockery on one palm and rapped on the door with the other. He'd asked Socrates to meet him here this morning, and for Summer's sake he hoped the young man hadn't arrived yet. There wouldn't be much conversation going on if he had.

Slowly, the door was dragged back, and there was Summer.

"Hi." She clutched a flimsy bathrobe across her chest as her face broke into a beaming smile. "The water heater works!"

She held the door open for him to pass through. "I left the fire on all night and I've just run the bath and it works!"

How someone could look so stunning, at this hour of the morning and without makeup, was beyond him. Her tousled mane of blonde hair fluffed around her face, and the pink flush of joy on her cheeks made her radiant. Her excitement at the simplicity of running hot water made his feelings of guilt from yesterday reignite. If only he could put her up in a hotel, pay for enough workers to get this job done in a week, then she wouldn't have to go through all this.

"I'm sorry." He backed toward the door. "I'll come back later. You can't let that precious hot water go to waste."

He bent to place the box on the floor, but the touch of her hand on his arm stopped him dead. His skin drank in the soft warmth of her fingers, the slight pressure of her body against his sparking a base desire. Unable to resist the swing of his gaze to hers, he took his fill of her delicate face and perfect lips, before reason reasserted itself and he remembered the distance he had to keep.

"It's alright." Her voice was lighter than the day before. "I'm the one who slept late. I can't believe it's nearly eight." She lifted her hand from his arm, but the imprint stayed warm. "What's in the box?"

As she leaned over, the soft fabric of the bathrobe slipped down to reveal the curve of a breast. His fingertips pulsed as he imagined how touching that dewy skin might feel, or even the length of her neck, the curve of her hip, the plane of her stomach...

He focused on the box. "A few things for breakfast."

As she stood, the smile she gave him almost knocked him sideways. It was the first time he'd seen her like this. Her eyes, her face, everything appeared softer. As if she wanted him to be here.

"Just give me a few minutes in the bath and I'll be right with you." Without waiting for him to reply, she moved through to the bathroom, maneuvering her way through the jammed door.

He thrust his hands into his pockets and turned to look anywhere except at the door. "I can wait outside."

"It's fine," she called. "Especially if you want to do something with all that lovely food."

Looking around the room for a place to put the makings for breakfast, he noticed the wooden chest in the corner, a purple scarf thrown over it.

A book and a magazine sat on top. Moving closer, he smiled as he noticed the book was an English/Greek dictionary—she was clearly trying to ensure her conversations with the locals wouldn't be one-sided. The magazine was some sort of real estate publication. It was open at a page of houses that all looked the same, each with a catchy title: "Entertainer's Delight," "Young Couple's Dream," "Suburban Stunner." He looked closer at one house that was circled. "Safe Anchorage" showed a plain brick house with no garden or trees.

Something pulled at his chest. Why should he care about her life on the other side of the world? It was clear from their conversation last night that money and material things were very important to her, and he'd had enough of women who valued possessions over people. Sure, he had plenty of money, but it had never been his motivation in business and never would be.

It was Caroline, all those years ago, who'd told him the story of the man who'd sold his soul to the devil for material things, and he'd always kept that close to his heart. She'd also given him the courage to be the man he wanted to be, not follow the dream his father had for him. If Summer wanted to live a safe life surrounded by belongings, why did it bother him?

Because *she* bothered him. Stirred him.

He collected the book and magazine to place them on the floor, and a photograph fluttered to the floor. It must have come from the box.

He picked it up and warmth gathered in his heart. It was the Caroline he remembered, locked in an embrace with a man. From what Caroline had told him, Summer knew very little about the life her mother had lived in Greece. He imagined Summer alone, holding the photograph that had lain in this house for the last thirty years, and wondering who this man in her mother's life had been. It must have been heartbreaking.

Carefully, he placed the book and the real estate magazine, with the page open as he'd found it, on the floor and tucked the photo in the middle.

He pulled the box to a sunny spot at the edge of the room, then began setting out breakfast. The morning was balmy, but a slight draft from the broken window reminded him he must get it fixed today.

"You slept well?" He raised his voice so she could hear him over the running water. Gazing across at the unmade bed, he imagined her in the sheets, warm in sleep; how the soft skin across the perfect curve of her back might feel against the length of his body...

And then the image changed to her lying there with another man, and he was startled by the green arrow that pierced his heart.

Their marriage would be over in a month.

"I did," she called. He could hear the squeak as she turned off the faucet. "Apart from those two love birds in the roof. They must have been at it all night."

He cleared his throat. "At it?"

"Nest building. They were scuffling around till about four this morning."

"I'll get Socrates to help me in the attic today."

Costa pulled out cups, glasses and plates, followed by watermelon, sweet bread, then cheese. A bag of coffee and a squat coffee pot were next, and he was glad to see the pensione owner had delivered the gas burner as promised. He moved to the lone faucet and filled the pot.

At intervals, the sound of water swirling in the next room sent his imagination to places it shouldn't have gone; how her body might look in the water, her lean shoulders caressed by bubbles, one slim brown leg tossed over the side.... He quickly spooned coffee, then sugar, into the pot, topped it with water and set it on the gas flame.

"Did you tell your father what you're doing for me?" Summer called. "Have you seen him much since you've been back?"

Costa picked oranges from the bowl and sliced into them with his army knife, the bloodred juice shocking him as it did every time. He licked the juice from his fingers and a warm memory of sitting in his family's orange grove stole into his heart.

"I haven't seen him today," he said. He paused. "I'll tell him when the time is right."

"Do you have brothers and sisters to visit while you're here?"

A swish-swish suggested she was soaping her body, creating bubbles that would lie sparkling on her skin, kissing crevices he fought not to imagine.

"No." He squeezed the juice into a glass then sliced another orange, refusing to look at the door that separated them. "They've all left the island. I have two brothers in Athens and a sister in Canada. I'm the eldest."

The chant in the distance of the *koulouri* man going door to door with his fresh bread heightened his senses further.

Something about the calm of the room, the call of the baker and the gentle rhythm of Summer in the bath made him stop what he was doing. He'd left his phone back at the hotel and no one, especially the annoying CEO of his property development company in Germany, knew where he was.

He couldn't remember the last time he'd done something as simple as make breakfast for someone. Either he ate at restaurants, or when he was back home in Switzerland, he had a housekeeper who took care of cooking.

He looked out the window, across to the brown hill he'd played on as a child. Even now, he could smell the wild oregano that covered the banks he used to slide down. Being here with someone who knew nothing of his life, who had no expectations of him, was liberating. A weight he hadn't known was there lifted from his shoulders.

"I'm nearly finished," Summer called. "Just going under now to rinse my hair."

The image of her naked body submerging into the ecstasy of deep, warm water, eyes closed, was enough to cause an involuntary groan to rake the back of his throat as he fought the want and need within him.

Now was not the time, and this was most definitely not the place, to allow those sorts of warring emotions to take over. He was on a focused mission. Renovate the house, then move on with his life. He had companies to buy, corporations to acquire.

"What made you all leave?" Summer called as a gurgle indicated she'd pulled the plug.

Costa busied himself with another orange in an attempt to push away the delicious image of her getting out of the bath. "Drive," he said. "Fear."

"Fear of wha—"

"*Koulooorriiiaaaaa*!!"

"Arrrrrrgghh!"

At her scream, he rushed into the bathroom and found Summer clutching a towel around herself, pointing at the window.

"A man!" she cried. "A man looked in the window!"

Her eyes were wide.

Costa grinned. "I see you've met Petro, the baker." He moved to the window and looked out. Petro was huddled over his basket of bread as though he'd been assaulted. Costa explained the situation and offered the poor old guy enough Euros to compensate for his load of bread, which lay scattered on the ground.

Was she really standing nearly naked, only inches from a Greek God leaning out her window? The racing of her heart should've been from the fright at seeing a strange face at the window, but now there was a more physical, immediate reason. The deep, throaty way Costa spoke to the baker made her blood heat, and as he leaned further out her window and his T-shirt rode higher up his back, her breath caught at the sight of his smooth, tan skin. How might his skin feel should her palm slide the entire length of him?

Even though he spoke in Greek, Summer could hear the amusement in the rich words of his native tongue. She pulled the towel tighter and tucked the end in securely. Costa reached into his pocket, pulled out some money and leaned out the window one more time before calling, "*Yah-sas*." He then turned around to face her, four giant bread knots in his hands, and Summer heard the reply, "*Yah-sas, Kirieh Nicoliedies*."

"Petro said to say he's very sorry to have looked in the

window. He knew someone was staying here, and he remembered the front door was broken, so he came around the back."

Summer grinned. "He obviously knows the village well. Did I scare him?"

The grin was returned. "Petro has seen many things in this village. Most people just reach out the window with their money for their morning *koulouri*, so he's seen plenty in his time."

Hair dripping and feeling distinctly uncomfortable half naked in front of Costa, Summer was about to suggest he leave so she could dry herself when there was a knock on the door.

"That'll be Socrates," he said as he made his way through to the next room. "You get ready, then we can get down to some serious work."

It was a little difficult for Summer to "get ready." All her clothes were still in the other room where there was a lengthy conversation going on between Costa and Socrates. Bathrobe tied firmly and her hair in a towel, she finally emerged from the bathroom.

"Hello." She held up one hand in a wave. Socrates, bless his heart, darted his gaze around the room. Anywhere but on her.

"Socrates doesn't speak English, Summer." Costa's burning eyes were fixed firmly above her neck. "He's very excited you'll help him with his song lyrics, though." He seemed to suddenly realize her predicament. "Coffee's made." He indicated two tiny cups on top of the box. "I'll show Socrates downstairs so he can get started. We need one of the rooms ready so I can move in tonight. I'll be back up in a moment."

When they left, Summer hurriedly dressed in shorts and a T-shirt. The flutter of excitement she'd felt when she awoke that morning returned to her stomach as she picked up the tiny cup of coffee.

This was truly her house. In all its tumbledown glory, it had initially seemed an insurmountable obstacle, but with Costa's help it just might turn into something amazing.

Now all she needed to do was find out what was motivating him to do this. She'd taken in the watch and designer boots, and she'd heard the guarded tone in his voice whenever she asked about his life. There was much more to this man who was supposedly in need of a translation job.

She looked out across land he must've played on as a child. What benefit could any of this possibly have for him?

Summer spent the rest of the morning and early afternoon sanding upstairs window frames, ready for the new glass Costa hoped to install later in the day.

Despite enjoying the physical work and friendly greetings from people as they passed along the lane, she was acutely aware of the low murmur down in the lean-to as Costa worked with Socrates. Knowing he was only a few feet away sent a secret thrill through her.

It was odd to have others in her house, especially strange to have men. At the commune, she and her mom had shared with other single mothers and children, and she'd been uncomfortable around men. Of course, she'd had boyfriends, but always just the dating kind, never the getting-their-feet-under-the-table kind.

Since she'd left the commune at seventeen, she'd always preferred her own company, but in ten years had never found a place that fitted, and she'd moved more than she'd admit.

Of course, money was the problem. Paying rent meant

lining someone else's pockets, never leaving enough to save for a deposit of her own. As soon as she closed on the house back in Brentwood Bay, she'd buy two cats, one fluffy and one sleek, and she'd live there with them forever.

While some of her friends were happy to move in with boyfriends who had their own house, she wanted her first real home to be just hers. It was ironic that she'd had to secure a husband before her dreams could take shape.

Looking around now, she allowed herself a sliver of hope that this place might finally be the answer to her dreams. If she could do what the council required, and sell it for a good profit, then "Safe Anchorage" would be hers. A house with a piece of lawn and neighbors you said hello to as you both went to work, and a mailbox with her number on it. That's what all this hard work could mean.

Her thoughts brought her gaze around to where the real estate magazine sat back on top of the box in the corner. Tucked into the magazine was the photo from the box. Something had made her take it out again last night. The emotion it had initially sparked was at first replaced by sadness that she was in this place without her mom. However, now she found it strangely calming that she could pull the image out and look at it whenever she wanted to and happy memories of her mom floated into her heart.

On the box beside the magazine and her English/Greek dictionary were two plates covered with a bright red cloth that Yianni from the café had brought early this afternoon. A delicious aroma wafted to her. Ground beef spiced with...cinnamon, she guessed, and a beautiful salad crammed with plump black olives and slabs of feta cheese. Two green bottles of beer, droplets of condensation glistening on their sides, were also on the tray, and although she'd never normally drink in the middle of the day, her dry throat had other ideas.

"*Yah-sas,*" she called to Socrates as he prepared to go home for lunch and a siesta. Later this afternoon, she'd help him with the pronunciation of his song lyrics while Costa installed the glass, then Athina would come for help with her English exam after school.

The young man stopped. He seemed to be looking for Costa, who hadn't come up from the lean-to yet. Taking a step toward Summer, he spoke in very broken English as he batted the air with both hands. "Tomorrow I no work. Tomorrow you come, please? To church. Kirieh Nicoliedies tell." He moved to the door.

Summer frowned. "I don't understand, Socrates. It's fine if you have to go to church tomorrow, but I don't think there's any need for me to come too."

A sheepish smile and shrug indicated he didn't understand her. "Kirieh Nicoliedies tell. *Yah-sas.*" And he was gone.

When she finally heard the fall of Costa's boots as he came upstairs for lunch, Summer was eager to know how his plans were progressing.

"How's it all looking?" she asked as they carried their plates outside. Sitting down with her back to the wall, she popped on her sunglasses. The afternoon was warmer than yesterday, a heat shimmer dancing over the grass on the hill opposite.

"Great." He handed her a beer and a piece of bread. "Socrates has sealed up the bigger holes where water was getting in, and this afternoon he'll plaster the walls."

"Downstairs?"

"Yes. We had a closer look around and that's the most urgent thing. I'll be able to find a dry enough place to put that bedroll tonight. We also had a look in the ceiling at your two love birds. Socrates said that side of the house is quite weak. The hole where the birds are getting in needs strengthening with new boards and then sealed up. He'll need to do some repairs to the plaster and the roof up there pretty soon or water could damage the entire ceiling."

Horror filled her. "But he can't do that! The birds have a nest up there. We have to do something else. Find another way."

He was silent for a moment. "I can't see any other way unless we move the nest to a safer place. You need to get this place weathertight."

"Could you talk to him for me? Please. I know it seems silly, but I can't bear the thought they might have nested there for years, and I'd be taking their home away from them."

A tightness in his lips showed he didn't empathize with the plight of a couple of swallows. She'd leave it for now.

"I feel bad that I didn't ask Socrates to stay for lunch." She dipped her bread in the lime green olive oil at the side of her plate.

"He wouldn't have expected it." Costa sat down in the shade of an olive tree opposite, his back straight, legs out in front. "Most people in the village go home for a midday meal and after that a short siesta, then they go back to work until six or seven. It's a much later working day than in some cooler parts of Europe."

Summer sifted her fork through the meat on her plate. "What about you, though? Don't you have a siesta?"

He shifted on the dry grass and took a mouthful of ground beef and cheese. "This is delicious, don't you think?" he asked after finishing. "My mother used to make beautiful *pastitsio* like this in winter and spring. In late summer, when there are lots of eggplants around, it'd become moussaka."

He was avoiding her question, just as he did every time she asked him something about his life. Unfortunately for him, she wouldn't let it go this time.

"A siesta," she said again. "Why don't you have one now you're home?"

He looked over at her and seemed to weigh his words. His eyes had the distant, closed look he got when she pushed too hard. Normally fluent and ready to talk, he spoke with obvious reluctance. "I spend most of my time talking to people in Europe, Australia or the US. I'd be laughed out of town if I stopped in the middle of the day for a snooze."

"So I guess Yianni knew you wouldn't be going home for a midday meal."

He grinned. "I think this meal was more for you than me. Yianni's used to the summer tourists. They don't rest in the afternoon either."

"So, what do you do there, in Switzerland, or is it Germany?" She'd keep up the momentum. It didn't seem right that this was her husband and she knew so very little about him. Concentrating on her food, she hoped to appear less interested than she was.

He shrugged. "I'm involved in some companies. Travel a lot. Never in one place for long."

"Because you don't like to stay in one place?" As soon as she'd said it, she wondered if she'd delved too deep, become too personal, especially when she remembered his comments about his father and leaving the island.

He held the fork to his lips and paused before speaking. "Perhaps." He looked away across the valley. "If I'd wanted to stay in one place, I guess I'd never have left Lesvos."

"What would you have done if you'd stayed here?"

He laughed sharply, a short, hard chuckle. "The same thing the eldest son in our family has done for generations."

"Become Mayor of the area?"

"Exactly."

"And that's not how you could see yourself living your life?"

He turned his body a little to face her fully. "From a very young age, I knew I didn't want to be restricted, didn't want people telling me what I should do, where I should live. I guess I passed the same feistiness on to my brothers and sister because they have the same attitude about the island." Something sparked in his eyes.

"So how did your parents feel about that?"

He shrugged. "My mother understood—to a certain extent. Many of her friends' children left the island for work, but most will still come back to spend the summer here."

"And your father?"

"He's killing himself with anger." The sharp clink as he dropped his fork on the plate added an exclamation point to his words. He looked out across the orange grove. Deep grooves forming on his forehead. "He thinks I've discredited the family name and abandoned them. Throwing aside your birthright, what your family values and expects of you, how they define themselves, isn't considered honorable."

His face looked the way it had when they'd first met, impenetrable and aloof. She searched for something positive to say. "But the old men in the village don't hold it against you," she said, then hurried on with the logic she'd stumbled across. "I mean, they were all over you in the square that day."

Slowly, he nodded. "Yes, but their criteria for what constitutes success are completely different to what my father believes."

There was a long silence, another moment when Summer realized the distance between them.

She laid her fork down on her plate. "Socrates said something weird as he was leaving for lunch. Something about not being able to work tomorrow and that I should come to church." She laughed at the last word—she hadn't set foot inside a church since her aunt's death when she was seven.

Her mom had only wanted a small service at the funeral home.

"He said that?" A frown tightened his brow.

"Yes, and he said you'd explain."

For a heartbeat, he seemed to hesitate. "I almost forgot. You're invited to a wedding." His eyes flicked back to his plate.

"A wedding?" She pushed the sunglasses on top of her head as her stomach dipped.

"Yes. Socrates' sister is getting married tomorrow. The entire village usually goes, which will include Socrates, Takis and me, so there'll be no one to work on the house. Socrates asked me to invite you." His voice was flat and emotionless. He could have been reciting a grocery list.

Didn't he want her to go? Although it shouldn't, the thought hurt.

"I couldn't possibly."

Dark eyes captured hers. "Why not?"

She moved the remaining food around her plate. "Well, I don't know Socrates' sister."

"Yes. I realize your custom is probably just to invite family and maybe a few friends, but in this part of Greece we invite everyone in the village."

She thought about the clandestine, rushed ceremony they'd had for their wedding and cringed. "But I didn't bring anything suitable to wear." Part of her was intrigued, interested to see what a real Greek wedding would be like, but the other part wanted to stay as anonymous as possible.

"What about the dress you wore yesterday? You looked beautiful."

Time crashed to a halt as the air between them sparked. He'd noticed how she looked yesterday? He'd thought she looked beautiful? Air squeezed flat in her lungs and she had to force herself to take a breath.

"That dress with a shawl for the church will be fine." He looked out across the orchard. "There will be a feast in the village square afterwards, which will be much less formal."

"Where will I go? What time?" Her mouth grew dry at the thought of turning up all by herself.

"We can go together." He seemed more positive. "At two o'clock. I have some things I need to do in the morning, and I guess Socrates will be busy. Perhaps you'd like some time to yourself in your own home, thinking about where the kitchen things should go."

For a while, they ate in silence. Summer wondered how she could ask Costa more about himself, why he was spending so much time with her and why he didn't want her to go to the wedding. Because it embarrassed him that his own marriage was a sham? Because she wasn't part of the village?

The swallows were still busy, flying up and under the eaves with bits of grass and feathers. The sun was scorching now and a sense of release came over her. Whereas she'd normally be at work, racing from one patient to the next, forgetting to eat lunch and some days not even sure what the weather was like outside, today she felt alive.

CHAPTER SIX

*C*osta broke the silence. "If you're uncomfortable about going, I could make an excuse for you." Why had he told her about the wedding? He could've just kept quiet, but he knew her well enough by now to know she wouldn't let this rest.

He'd explained to Socrates that it wasn't a good idea to invite her, but his friend harbored a deep respect for anyone foreign and hadn't wanted her to feel left out. By now, people would've worked out who she was though, and Costa didn't want to risk her being told more about her mother than she might want to hear.

"No," she said. "I'd like to come. People have been so welcoming, and I guess I should have some local experiences before I go home."

Still feeling a reluctance he could only half explain, Costa nodded. At least he could keep an eye on her at the wedding. If he kept her by his side all day and avoided any of the older people who spoke English, he could minimize any problems. When she was on her own, he risked her meeting neighbors, or other villagers, who remembered things from Caroline's time. He didn't understand why Caroline had asked him not to tell Summer about her time here. Maybe the memories had still been painful, or maybe she'd thought Summer would have enough to deal with.

As far as he knew, Summer knew nothing about how her mother had come by the house, or why she'd stayed on the island so long, but he knew that once Summer learned one secret, she would learn them all, and he'd sworn he wouldn't let that happen. The biggest problem would be to keep her away from his father and any particularly unpleasant words he might have for her.

"You could wear the purple shawl for the church," he suggested. "The one I saw inside."

"Oh, that flower-child thing." Summer screwed up her nose. "It smells like an old opium den with all that incense from the box. It's just the sort of thing Mom would've worn, even recently. I wonder what made her leave it behind in a box in the attic?"

"You didn't approve of your mother's lifestyle, did you?" He wanted to understand the mixed feelings she seemed to have for her mom.

She placed her plate on the ground and clasped the tiki. He'd noticed she often did that when she spoke of her mom. "I used to think it was fine, interesting even," she admitted, her gorgeous blue eyes drilling into his. "But you know—you can't live in a vacuum; you can't always do things just because they might work for you when there are others to consider."

He frowned. "That makes it sound as though you feel your mother didn't consider what you needed."

"She didn't." She shrugged a slim shoulder. "Especially later on in her life. If Mom had an itch, she'd scratch it and to hell with everyone else."

Yeah, that was the Caroline he remembered.

"Part of me deep down admires that way of living to a degree," she said, "but another part of me has been hurt too many times by it."

"Do you think it made her happy? Drifting from place to place?"

"She always said so. She said the worst thing you could do in life was what was expected of you when it wasn't your dream. The only place she stayed for any length of time was when the town I'm living in now. I was born during those years, and when I was three months old, we started moving and didn't stop until I could make my own life at eighteen. I think there's a lot to be said for tradition, establishing relationships and sticking with them instead of flitting from one place to the next."

She may as well be talking about him. Caroline was the one who'd taught him to fight against tradition, and it had got him everything he'd wanted: houses in four countries, more money than he knew what to do with, and no obligations to anything...or anyone. Being settled and sacrificing dreams just to please others made his stomach turn.

"What?" She leaned forward, her gaze intent upon his face.

It felt uncomfortably as if she was reading his deepest thoughts.

He flitted. *He* avoided his past.

Shifting his shoulders against the olive tree, he said, a little too coolly, "I don't know what you mean."

She sat back, her lashes lowering briefly. "You were frowning as if you didn't agree with what I said."

She was so direct. "I didn't mean to." He was sorry for the snub that had clearly hurt her. He wanted to get closer, not push her further away. "I don't understand why you'd be so against that particular lifestyle."

"Is that the way you live? Moving from place to place?"

"I spend quite a lot of time in a number of places. I'm inspired by different cultures and energized by meeting all sorts of different people. Having a lifestyle like your mom's did appeal to me hugely. I couldn't think of anything worse than being stuck in the same place."

She looked away from him, settling the dark glasses back over her eyes.

"If my mother hadn't been so committed to her 'lifestyle', she might be sitting here today instead of me."

"Ouch!"

Summer held out her hand and looked at the red raw knuckles. Sanding window frames most of the afternoon had left her tired and restless, and the dust was causing her lungs to work harder than they should. She'd decided not to wear her wedding ring when she was doing this sort of work. If they did happen to get a visit from immigration, she could easily explain the lack of a ring away. And it was sitting out in the open on her bedside table.

The back-and-forth rhythm of conversation downstairs suggested Socrates and Costa were still working, but she knew they'd be up shortly to put glass in the windows.

Lunch had ended on a tense note. And threatening tears had caused her to clam up.

She'd felt a twist of irritation at Costa's comments. What right did he have to judge her and the relationship she'd had with her mom? From what he'd told her, his relationship with his father was almost nonexistent.

"Hello?"

A young girl stood at the window, her glossy black hair flowing freely around her shoulders. "Are you Summer?" She spoke in near perfect English and smiled tentatively. About sixteen, she had a sweet face.

"Yes, I am." Summer grinned. "And you must be Athina."

She let the girl in through the now fully functioning door, and after washing her hands at the faucet, they headed out the back.

"I'm sorry I don't have a table and chairs." Summer offered Athina a seat on one of two large stones at the side of the house. The stones held the sun's warmth, and it seeped through her tired muscles. "I'm not here for long, but I hope I can help with what you need."

The girl's face lit up, her dark eyes sparkling. "Thank you so much." She pulled books from a bright pink Hello Kitty bag. "When Papa said Kirieh Nicoliedies would help me, I was overjoyed. I couldn't believe he was back and knew someone who could work with me on my English."

"Kirieh Nicoliedies." Summer said the name carefully, remembering the way she'd heard the old men use it in the square. "Why do people call him Kirieh when his name is Costa?"

Athina's smile was puzzled. "Kirieh?" she said the word slowly. "It means...Mister."

For a second it seemed logical that a girl Athina's age would call him Mister, but why would Socrates, and Yianni at the *kafenion,* call him that, and the old men too?

"But most people would call each other by their first names, wouldn't they?" She didn't want to pry, but struggled to understand.

"Everyone calls him Mister," Athina said matter-of-factly. "I guess it's because of who he is."

Because of who he is?

"Are you his girlfriend?"

Summer's breath stalled. Of course, people were going to ask questions. So why didn't she have a ready answer?

"He's... ah... he's very special to me. We're renovating this house together."

A shy smile curved the girl's lips. "There's a rumor in the village that you're already married, but I don't believe it because Kirieh Nicoliedies would have a big wedding in Athens or in Los Angeles, and it hasn't been in the papers."

He hadn't mentioned living in Los Angeles, but that might explain his very good English, and why would his marriage be in the papers? He'd mentioned his family had been mayor of this area for generations, so maybe that was it.

"Are you coming to the wedding tomorrow? Eleni and Makis have been together since high school, so everyone's really excited to see them finally married."

Summer smiled back at Athina. "Do you think it would be okay if I come? I've never even been inside a Greek Orthodox Church, but I'd love to."

"Of course, you must. Everyone is excited that Kirieh Nicoliedies will come. He doesn't come back to the island very often, so it will be very special."

"*Yah-sou*, Athina." Summer turned to see Costa standing in the doorway.

Her stomach leapt at the sight of him. His brow beaded with moisture and his hair glossy and damp, he walked over to them, and Summer noticed a fine white dust on the hairs of his arms. *Her* dust from *her* house. This time her stomach fluttered and wouldn't stop.

Athina leapt to her feet blurting something in Greek. If Summer wasn't mistaken, a blush covered the tan on her cheeks.

Costa moved across and kissed both cheeks of the awestruck girl. It was the same kind of reaction Summer had seen in the village square.

She tilted her head as if the only interesting things were Athina's schoolbooks. He was her pretend husband. He was doing her a huge favor so she could get what she wanted before they parted ways. She had no claim on him and was sure he wouldn't want her to.

He turned to Summer and suddenly *she* felt awestruck. The fluttering shifted lower, sending bolts of something delicious to her core.

"Isn't Athina's English amazing?"

"It sure is. Where did you learn, Athina?"

"We learn English from a very young age and many of us will go to extra lessons at private language schools. It's pretty easy with Netflix and YouTube and a ton of apps to help."

For a moment, Summer imagined how different and difficult it must have been for Caroline here back in the nineties. It would've been much harder for her to adapt and assimilate in the village.

"Kirieh Nicolidies," Athina said as she turned toward Costa, her cheeks blooming pink. "Thank you so much for arranging these lessons with Ms. Adams. I can't thank you enough."

Costa and Athina continued speaking in English, and Summer was struck by the impact that Costa was having on Athina, so similar to the reactions of the old men in the coffee shop.

What was this power he had over people? It was clear what it was for her—an intense physical reaction to everything about him. But now there was something else. Something about this man. Something other people knew, and she didn't.

Something she was going to find out.

CHAPTER SEVEN

When she opened the kitchen door to a knock the next afternoon, Summer had to keep her jaw tight to stop her mouth falling open.

If she'd thought her body did strange things at seeing Costa near naked the day before, it was nothing compared to the double somersault half pikes in her belly when she pulled the door wider to reveal him in a stunning black suit. It was as if he'd stepped from a magazine spread, and her breath faltered.

"Are you ready?" His gaze grazed her from top to toe.

His suit and shirt probably both came from the same designer as the boots she'd noticed yesterday, in which case his outfit probably cost more than her car back home. The stark white shirt touched the mocha skin of his neck, and she caught the subtle tang of musk. Not the commercial smell from a bottle, but the aroma of warm male body. Inside, her stomach swooped.

"You look beautiful." He spoke slowly, and she tried not to concentrate on his words or the spark that was zinging between them. Instead, she smoothed the pink shift dress around her hips and draped the mauve scarf about her shoulders as she stepped into the warming sunlight.

"Thank you," she said shyly. This man had the ability to make her forget how to think.

The dress was probably a little tighter than she would've liked for church, but it was the smartest thing she had in her suitcase that didn't need ironing.

Costa had stressed the need to wear something around her shoulders for the church, and the scarf was the only thing she had. She'd washed it in the tub the night before and left it out to dry. Thankfully, it now smelled less like a crystal and tarot card shop and the thought that her mother probably wore it while walking these same village paths sent a warm spiral through her. The jade tiki sat as it always did, cool and soothing on her breastbone.

Costa was quiet for a moment and then asked, "Have you ever been to a Greek Orthodox church?"

"No, but I'm looking forward to it."

She'd promised herself she'd just attend the church service, then quietly make an excuse so she didn't have to stay for the celebrations later. Agreeing to go to a church of all places, where she knew no one and didn't understand the language, was one thing. Having to be face-to-face with a proper marriage and the beauty that surrounded it would be too difficult.

She'd been carried away at the thought of spending more time with Costa, but now that a level of tension had developed between them, it seemed like a ridiculous idea. She'd leave so he could relax and have a good time. Remembering the reaction of the men in the *kafenion,* and also Athina the day before, she didn't doubt Costa would be surrounded by people most of the day. It would be easy to slip away. During lunch yesterday she'd sensed he wasn't overjoyed about her going either, but she could hardly back out now. Socrates had beamed when Costa explained she'd be there, and Athina had said she looked forward to seeing her.

They walked up the cobbled hill in silence, Summer glad she'd worn her flat sandals rather than high heels. The afternoon sun shone hotter than the day before, and she hoped she wouldn't be sweating by the time they got there.

The lessons had gone well last night—first Athina, then Socrates. She didn't get a chance to question Athina further about Costa, as he was always in earshot while putting the glass in the windows. When she and Athina had moved to the front of the house to catch the last of the sun, he'd inconveniently moved windows too. Of course, he had to be close by when she was helping Socrates, as she sometimes had trouble making herself understood—but it was frustrating. Athina's words *'Because of who he is'* echoed in her mind.

But that was then. Now, it was the unmistakable charge sparking between them that was the real cause of Summer's anxiety.

As they passed it, she noticed the *kafenion* was shut, as were several other stores around the square, but tables had been pushed together and it was clear there would be a celebration here later.

"Are the stores shut for the wedding?"

"Yes. They wouldn't be if it were the middle of summer, but the tourist season hasn't started yet. It's a chance for everyone to celebrate together." He smiled, and she felt it all the way to her toes.

"Will your father be there?" She presumed that if she had been invited, then so would the mayor.

Instantly the smile fell away. "Probably."

"It would be nice to meet him."

Costa stopped abruptly and turned to her. She couldn't see his eyes behind the dark glasses, but it was clear from his hard-set jaw something was wrong.

"He doesn't speak very good English," he said roughly and began walking again. He was hiding something?

"You could translate for me."

"It's not a good idea." His stride quickened.

That patronizing tone again. Wrapping the shawl tight around her shoulders, she hurried after him.

"Costa?" He kept walking. "Costa, I think it's time you gave me some answers." She'd caught up with him but was almost running as she tried to match his enormous stride.

"Is it because I'm a foreigner? If you explain to him I want to restore the house in the traditional way and then leave, won't that be enough? I don't want to change anything here. You know I just need to make some money and have my own dream home."

He stopped again. This time she was surprised to see he was angry, both sides of his jaw flexing at the same time. "Why is everything always about money with you? I don't think we've had a single conversation without you mentioning how having money will make your life perfect, solve all your problems, and how not having money messed up your relationship with your mom. Why do you obsess over it so much? I can't understand how someone whose mother lived a life without the need for material things can be so shallow."

He looked away as the words smacked into her, a body blow that almost left her staggering.

Almost.

"You," she said, forcing herself not to point a finger, "have no idea what my mother was really like, and you obviously have no concept of what it means to have no money. You've seen in the last few days how not having money can limit someone's dreams, so don't lecture me!"

At first he said nothing, but the slight turn of his head toward her indicated she'd surprised him. He started to speak, paused, then said, "I understand that your mother lived by some important principles. If she moved here to a different country and taught the children of another culture, she must have had compassion. You've told me she carried on living that lifestyle when she returned home, so it must've been extremely important to her. I'm just wondering how your views can be so different."

She breathed through her nose and started to speak, but her lip wobbled so she took another breath. "My mother—" The word caught sharp in her throat, but she continued. "My mom had breast cancer, but she refused all conventional treatment."

His jaw dropped and brow furrowed. She'd wanted to shock him out of his smug judgments, but more importantly, she'd wanted him to understand where her mother's "lifestyle" had led them both.

"Summer, I—"

Blinking quickly, she held up a hand. "Let me finish."

The corners of his mouth turned down, and he pushed the sunglasses up on his head. Even though anger vibrated through her, she felt a pang of regret at the shock in his eyes.

"They found it early," she said, hardly believing she was telling him. "Early enough that she could have had surgery, undergone state-of-the-art treatments for both the short and long term. She started the presurgical treatment, and I made plans to start a second job to save for a new drug. I was so, so hopeful that it would mean we'd have some quality time together. But then she stopped the treatment and called off the surgery without telling me." A sharp pain constricted her throat, and she fought to swallow.

He took a step toward her, and for a moment, tears prickled behind her eyes. Then she remembered what he'd said, and the words came easily. "While I was working, instead of being at the hospital like I thought she was, my mother was being chanted over and drinking herbs all day. If she'd been up front with me, I might have understood why she wanted to go that route, but by the time she told me, it was too late. It was so like her to take charge of her treatment like that, but..."

She pulled in a breath, wanting to make him understand, but not trusting the tremor that was building behind her words. "I could have done it, you know. I could have earned more. I *should* have earned more. At the very least, I should have convinced her it wouldn't matter how much it cost, I would find the money, but she gave up on us. Gave up on us finally having a real mother/daughter relationship. The thing I'd wanted. Craved so badly."

He reached out with one hand, and his strong fingers gripped her elbow. His touch was as firm as she'd imagined it would be, not tentative or questioning. Her mind wanted to shake him away. Her body wouldn't move.

Her voice strengthened as she said, "I know money doesn't buy everything—but it helps. When I finally had enough, my mother wouldn't accept it and it was too late." The words tasted bitter as she forced herself to say them. "She believed she could heal herself. That positive thinking and having a great mindset would make a difference. In the end...nothing could help her."

She swallowed, knowing she'd said all this as a challenge, daring him to tell her she was wrong. "How can I understand any of this?" She swept her free arm wide, and the scarf slid to the cobbled street. "The hippies, the alternative lifestyle. The fact she owned a house in Greece that could have funded her treatment ten times over if she'd sold it. Costa, how can I be anything but cynical when it's the same principles you talk so admiringly of that killed my mother?"

She wrenched her elbow from his hold to pick up the scarf, tears making the cobbles waver in front of her eyes.

As she righted herself, his warm hands clutched her shoulders.

The power of his touch made her take a step back, and she yielded to the security of a wall behind her. She hardly dared look up, didn't want to let herself go.

"I'm so sorry, Summer. I shouldn't have said those things about money. I had no right to judge you." Regret swam in his eyes and pain laced his voice.

She lifted her chin and felt the pull of him. She wanted to be held, wanted his hands to caress every part of her, wanted him to take away the pain.

Slowly, he drew her to him, his potent gaze holding her paralyzed. More than anything, she wanted to drown in him, forget the monumental task that had brought her here, forget the lengths she'd had to go to make this work, and succumb to his power and the tangled emotions he aroused in her.

Only a breath away, his warm male scent willed her closer, but just as her body melted she drew back. A secret power in him, something she didn't understand, caused her to lean back into the wall, her legs threatening to buckle. "This is not a good idea," she said, trying to keep the tremor from her voice and dragging the scarf between them like a barrier. "I don't need comforting, just some understanding."

As Summer drew back from him, Costa cursed his impulses, the searing reminder of what he wanted. Every part of him burned to drag her close so he could truly touch her, take away the pain that washed across her face.

He'd been around far too many women who were seduced by money, and it had disappointed him that Summer appeared to be one of them. Now he knew the reason why it was so important to her, guilt rushed through him at his quick judgment.

Was it guilt for the secret he kept that caused every nerve ending to pull him to her? He shouldn't have this desire for her, and he mustn't act on it. Things were complicated enough.

"I'm sorry." His tone was rough, but he carefully released her shoulders, their delicacy imprinted on his palms. "I should never have pushed you like that, it was unforgivable. You've been through so much with your mother, and it's not for me to question your priorities."

Moving to the side, she avoided his gaze and began walking. "Parent/child relationships are anything but simple."

A pointed comment. What right did he have to talk of her mother's qualities when his views clashed so badly with his father's? If he could just tell her what her mother was *really* like, how those attributes Summer so despised had encouraged him to become what he wanted to be, then maybe he could help her heal those painful memories. The battle between the promise he'd made to Caroline and his need to soothe Summer's grief clashed within him.

He lengthened his stride to catch up to her. Their harsh words had affected her physically. She walked with a stoop and had the purple scarf drawn tight around her shoulders, despite the warmth of the day. He needed to say something, put right the hurt he'd caused.

"I think what you're doing with the house is great," he said, working hard to find the words to really convey what he meant. "By returning to where your mother spent some time, you're celebrating part of her life. I'm sure she'd be very proud of the things you're achieving here."

Summer kept walking, but her head lifted as they neared the church.

She said nothing, so he continued. "Maybe being here and completing this project will make you feel closer to her."

They were directly outside the church and she stopped abruptly and turned to him. "Let's get one thing clear." Her voice was full of emotion, her fragile cheekbones tinged pink. "I'm here to sell this wretched house so I can finally make some money. That's it. That's all." A hand sat on her hip as if in defiant emphasis. "It might mean nothing to you—and it meant nothing to my mother—but, Costa, whether you like it or not, money means freedom. I've never been free. I've lived from hand to mouth, from one struggle to the next, my whole life. Well, I'm sick of being trapped, and now that my mom's gone, I can finally live the life I choose. And that's going to take money."

Costa pulled up short. He didn't want to believe her. It was the fifty-foot wall she'd built around herself speaking—that's what was making her focus on the money. He'd glimpsed the real woman behind that wall and he wanted things to be different this time. It was as if something he'd thought unattainable had suddenly been within his grasp, but then with her last words it had been ripped away again. For the last ten years he'd been surrounded by women with similar values and a belief that money solved everything; maybe he'd been a fool to think differently about her.

He'd learned plenty of things while making inane conversation on super yachts with women only interested in his share portfolio and accompanying status-hungry women to fashion shows who only wanted to hold his wallet, not his hand. The next time he started a relationship it would be with a woman who saw *him*, wanted to be *with him*. Even if he were dirt poor and they lived in a shack, she'd look at him every morning with love in her eyes.

Her concern about the damned swallows was the only thing that suggested Summer wasn't always money hungry and that she had a whole lot more to her that she kept carefully guarded. That and the way she looked when she held the jade pendant around her neck. Perhaps acknowledging the spiritual and emotional side of her was too confronting. Whatever her true feelings, it was clear she wasn't going to let him get close, even if he'd wanted to.

His secret hung like a brittle curtain between them. If only he could be honest with her and help her understand that her mother inspired so many to live their dreams. To live lives not bound by tradition but becoming the person they were meant to be. Maybe then some of Summer's other barriers might come down too. But instead, he'd fulfill his promise to a dying woman. Even though he was drawn to Summer in ways he didn't understand, he'd carry on with the task Caroline had assigned him, and he'd make sure Summer returned to the States with the money she craved.

They stood at the bottom of the church steps. Every second person stopped to greet him, and she had no choice but to stand there and wait.

Her hair blew across her dusky lips, and she oozed discomfort, her scarf pulled tight around her shoulders. When he finally extracted himself from a group of old classmates, he put his hand on the small of her back and steered her up the steps. She didn't resist and when he leaned in and whispered, "I'm sorry," her muscles relaxed beneath his hand.

He chose seats at the back of the church, and although he was aware of people turning around to look at him, he concentrated on Summer.

As he leaned in to whisper again, the heady scent of jasmine and a spring breeze invaded his senses. She looked straight ahead but cocked her head toward him slightly.

"I shouldn't have been so judgmental," he said as the chanters took their positions at the side of the altar. "What you do with the house is your own business. I want you to know that whatever you do, I'm here to help."

She didn't move for a moment, didn't answer, and then... a slight nod of her head.

~

It could've been the lyrical chanting of the men at the altar. Perhaps it was the sight of the bride and groom, their wedding crowns linked with a simple ribbon. Or maybe it was the warm sincerity of Costa's apology. But something caused the tears to well and spill down Summer's cheeks.

She'd never told anyone what she'd just told him. In fact, she wasn't even sure she'd acknowledged it herself until she'd tossed the terse words out. It wasn't his fault he'd had the bad luck to be landed with her in this state, and she really had to stop being angry at him.

Although she looked straight ahead, she sensed his very physical presence beside her. Every now and then, the fabric of his trousers brushed the bare skin on her leg and his heat warmed her. As she sat beside him now, the air soft with the scent of incense, it occurred to her that she'd seen him in practically every state of dress. What would it be like to see every part of his body? To touch him? Feel his warm hands stroking—

She swallowed and sat straighter. Not the sort of thoughts to be having about someone you had just been angry at, especially not in a church.

Turning her head slightly, she was momentarily shocked by the sight of him. She'd expected indifference toward the ceremony and the same haughtiness she'd seen in the last couple of days. Instead, with his glasses removed and his huge dark eyes soft and focused on the couple at the front, the hint of a smile curling his full lips, she could see an intensity that hadn't been obvious before. The thought that a real marriage could move him sent a river of warmth to her core.

The ceremony went on for the best part of an hour, so by the time it was finished and Costa stood up and suggested they should move out of the church, her mood was more relaxed than when they'd arrived.

As they emerged into the sunshine, Costa was stopped by numerous people and even Summer was greeted by Yianni from the café and half of Socrates' family. After struggling with greetings and small talk, she was relieved to see Athina standing by herself a short way off. She indicated to Costa she was joining Athina under the shade of an oleander.

While chatting with her young student, she watched Costa and the women of the village who were practically lining up to greet him. He must be seen as quite a catch—a boy from the village who was obviously successful overseas. Suddenly, a sharp thought pierced her. Did he have someone waiting for him at his home in Switzerland?

She'd presumed, with the speed he suggested marriage, that no other wife existed anywhere, but she hadn't even asked about a partner, or children. She didn't even know how old he was. The dusting of gray at his temples suggested he could be in his late thirties, but she had no real idea.

Her thoughts had almost consumed her when she heard Athina say, "And this is Costa's father."

Standing in front of them was a silver version of Costa— the same straight spine, the same unflinching gaze.

"Kirieh Nicoliedies," Summer said, remembering the way he should be addressed as she extended her hand. At least she knew one polite word of greeting. "Yah-sas. I'm Summer Adams. From America."

The older man stayed rigid, hands by his sides, the only movement a slight nod of his head as he said, "I know who you are. I hear you're planning to renovate a house in our

101

village. I hope you understand that there are strict rules regarding what can be changed about our buildings."

If there was one thing Summer's mother had taught her, it was how to read people. This man was not happy, and now that Athina had turned to talk to someone else, Summer realized she was alone with him. Had he heard about the marriage? She clasped her hands together, glad she hadn't put her wedding ring on this morning.

Remembering Costa's comments about foreigners destroying the atmosphere of the village, she spoke to reassure him. "I'm doing the renovations," she said. "Exactly as they should be done. Of course, I couldn't do it without Costa. He's not only translating, he's helping me do the work."

The old man's eyes stayed steady despite the surrounding skin puckering in a squint. He spoke slowly, his tone cold. "Still under the spell, then," he said. "After all these years, nothing has changed." Summer looked around to see if he was talking to someone else. His words made no sense to her.

"I'm sorry?" She tried another smile to reassure him. "I don't understand." She looked over to Costa. It was obvious he'd seen her with his father and was trying to extricate himself from the group. She breathed a sigh of relief as he joined them.

"Papa," he said, nodding to the older man. "I see you've met Summer."

Mr. Nicoliedies said a few words in Greek before Costa interrupted him.

"I think it would be more polite if we spoke in English, for Summer's sake."

His father's short exhalation indicated he didn't agree with his son, and the tension in the air seemed ready to ignite.

"I am sure you would rather speak in English," his father said sharply, "but it would be very nice for once if you could remember who you are." He turned to Summer. "I am sorry, young lady, that you are caught up in the old arguments of a father and son. You might like to ask Costa why there is such a gulf between us."

What on earth could she say? She felt guilty for not being able to speak Greek, but it seemed unfair of his father to chastise Costa for speaking English.

Costa touched her arm as if to reassure her. "This is not something we need to discuss in front of Summer, surely, Papa."

"Discuss?" The older man's face contorted as if in an effort to contain anger. "You and I have discussed nothing for *years*. If it hadn't been for outsiders coming into our village and enticing our young people away, you and I might have spent far more time *discussing* things."

Now Costa's hand moved to the small of her back, the breadth of his palm a stamp of protection. "No one is to blame, Papa, especially not Summer."

His father stood straighter and seemed to remember some sense of social decorum. "Of course not," he muttered, "of course not. I am sorry, Summer. Sometimes I forget myself."

She captured his gaze then and was startled that, instead of anger, his gaze spoke of long-held sorrow.

No matter how much Costa had wanted to avoid a meeting between Summer and his father, it had always been going to happen. He should have told her everything earlier, tried to make her understand why he had such a hard time hearing her speak of her mother the way she did.

As he watched his father walk away and join a group of men at the side of the church, the knot of regret he always felt when they were together burned inside him.

"Costa, what on earth was that about?" Summer asked, eyes wide. "Does he know about our marriage? Was that why he seemed so angry?"

Costa's stare followed his father. "The only thing he knows is that I'm back on the island and helping you to renovate your house. That is enough."

She waited until his gaze moved back to her. "I thought your father knew about you working with me? It sounded as though he hated the idea."

"There are some things I need to tell you," he said, looking around. "Most people will stroll back to the square for the feast. We could sit on the hill opposite so we can see when it's time for the festivities to start. We can talk on the way."

Would she be too fragile to hear this? Given their conversation of an hour ago, perhaps he should try to delay, but as he spent more time with her, it was getting harder and harder not to tell her the whole truth.

"My father knew your mother." He glanced across to judge how she might take this. He wanted to hold her, protect her, shield her from the inevitable blow while she came to terms with the truth.

"I know. You told me your father asked you to do the translating for me when he was approached by my mother's lawyer."

"No, that's not how it happened." Costa removed his jacket and flung it over his shoulder. "If your mother's lawyer had contacted my father, we wouldn't both be standing here."

Her brow drew together. "But I thought—"

"You thought, because my father was the mayor, he must have known of the arrangement for me to help with translating."

She nodded.

"My father knew I was helping with some translation work, but initially he didn't know it was for you."

She stopped and lifted her shoulders in a shrug. Her scarf slipped, so she grabbed it and tied it in a knot. "I still don't understand."

He took a breath and held it for a moment, judging carefully how much he could tell her without breaking his promise. He saw the trust in her eyes and wanted to do everything possible to help her understand. "Your mother taught a class in the village school. She was here for a year and had a huge impact on the children." Everything he said was true. Although he couldn't tell her the whole truth, he wouldn't lie to her.

Summer took a step back so he reached for her and drew her up onto a knoll covered in new grass. It was her wrist he held, not her hand—its delicate size reminding him of how careful he needed to be, but the pulse beneath his fingers reminding him how close to her he wanted to be.

When they were sitting, he let go and continued. "She spoke a lot about individual choice, about freedom."

Summer nodded. "Yes, that would be right."

"To many of the children in the village, she was a revelation. She spoke of traveling the world, experiencing as much as possible and never settling for what society expected."

She plucked at the grass. "And those weren't popular views?"

"For some parents they were, but not for mine. Although, it was only after she'd left that my father blamed her, said she was the reason so many children chose to leave the village."

"No wonder he hates me."

"He doesn't hate you. He just sees you as a representation of the things your mother believed in."

Summer let out her tinkling laugh. "But you know that's

not true. Couldn't you tell him what I'm like? That I'm a materialistic heathen who wants the comforts of home." She smiled at him then, and he realized that what he'd told her hadn't affected her at all.

"You're not upset?"

She undid the scarf and let it fall to the ground, the milky skin of her shoulders pulling his gaze from her face. The pink dress she wore hugged her curves and rode up above her knees when she was sitting down. He dragged his gaze back from her perfect legs as she spoke.

"Not at all. I became used to people making fun of my mother, her mismatched flowing skirts and numerous necklaces. For a time she wore no footwear, even in winter, and little kids would point at her in the streets. I guess I just got used to it."

"Did you ever feel proud of her?" He was pushing, but he was so relieved he wasn't going to have to explain further that he took the risk.

Resting elbows on her knees, Summer rubbed her hands on her face, then turned to him. "Yes, I did."

She smiled at him and continued. "When I was about ten, she retrained and became a midwife. It meant ridiculous hours, but living in the commune always meant someone was around to look out for me. The people of the community loved her. She was so relaxed and yet passionate about women having choices in childbirth. She inspired me to want to become a nurse too."

She reached down the neck of her dress and pulled out the jade pendant he'd noticed on the first day. "This was given to her by an old Maori woman when Mom worked in New Zealand. She went there when I was in college. Mom saved the life of the woman's daughter and her baby in childbirth. The woman said the person who wore this would always be blessed."

He looked at her face, the strength and the pride in her eyes, and he didn't doubt it. She was like no woman he'd ever met, pulling no punches, communicating what she believed in, not what someone wanted to hear.

"Oh, look." She stood and pointed across to the *kafenion* in the distance. "Everyone's gathering for the feast. You should go."

"I don't know if I will." He thought of the fuss everyone had made in the village.

"I won't go without you," she said, smiling. "Although if you think it would make a mockery of your father, I won't go."

Costa stood up beside her. It was time he stopped running from his past. Time he celebrated his life as Caroline would've wanted. If Summer Adams could acknowledge her mother's faults head on and be determined to move forward, then why couldn't he do the same with his past?

CHAPTER EIGHT

ot an inch of Summer's plate could be seen under glossy spit-roast lamb, golden fried pota-toes and a huge Greek salad. As people took their seats, the sound of children laughing and families chatting danced in the breeze. She held out her glass to Costa who poured her some wine. He'd been speaking to a large group at the next table but now sat next to her.

"I haven't done this for years." His eyes were bright, boyish, and her heart missed a beat. The dozen people at their table were all deep in intense and noisy conversation, but he was focused only on her. "I hated it, you know, coming to these sorts of things when I was a kid."

She looked at a group of small boys chasing each other between the tables, grins on their chubby faces and squealing in delight. They didn't look as though they were having a bad time. She nodded to them as she spoke. "A little like those poor little souls."

He looked over and grinned. "Maybe I was older when I disliked it. It's funny, but I don't remember doing anything like this since I left the island—a whole community gathering."

She tilted her head. "You don't have friends and a community in Switzerland?"

"I have friends all over and a few in the village from school. I live in an apartment in Geneva, near the airport so I can come and go easily." He shrugged a strong shoulder. "I don't know many people because I'm hardly ever there."

"I couldn't think of anything worse." She reached for the olive oil. "I suppose I've always been around people so much it just feels natural. Even though it bothers me sometimes, it's nice to know people are there if you need them and if they need you." He turned his head at some laughter from an adjacent table, and she asked the question swirling in her mind. "Do you have someone special waiting for you in Switzerland?"

Mortified that she'd just tossed such a loaded question into the conversation as if it was a random thought, Summer concentrated on her plate.

Costa's laugh was like manna from heaven. "Hell, no."

While she could barely contain a squeal of happiness at his response, she hadn't been expecting *such* a strong dismissal of the idea. The breath she'd been holding slipped out slowly.

"Work's the most important thing in my life right now. It wouldn't be fair to ask someone to always wait for me or follow me around the world."

That comment didn't make her feel any better. No wonder he'd found it so easy to suggest a marriage of convenience. He had no room in his life for any other kind.

"And what about you? Do you have someone back in the States?"

"No." Why couldn't she sound as dismissive as he had? "Focusing on mom while she was sick meant I didn't have time for relationships. And now the home I have the deposit on is my focus."

"Tell me about your dream home." His eyes were warm, interested.

Summer placed her knife and fork at the side of her plate. Thinking about the house she'd first shown her mom in a real estate catalogue made her heart skip. "I found it when Mom's diagnosis became terminal, and I wanted a secure place to look after her— the first home of our own. Somewhere we could make our peace with each other. I paid the deposit, but then I had to get an extension on the closing date on compassionate grounds. I don't think the bank will extend it again."

"What's it like? The house?"

She smiled so wide her jaw hurt. "It's new, in a brand new suburb." Contentment curled through her as she thought of the house she was determined would become her home. "I guess it doesn't have much soul yet, but by the time I've finished, it will."

"When you've hung all your Greek ornaments around the walls." His dark chocolate eyes danced.

Looking down at her plate, Summer's cheeks warmed. He had been listening to her.

"Why *that* house?"

"I suppose I'm at a time in my life when I need some security. It feels—"

"Safe?"

She nodded as he held her gaze, and the real estate title of the house skipped through her mind, *Safe Anchorage.*"Yes, I guess it does."

"Costa," a young woman said in an American accent as she approached the table. "I didn't think you'd come." Two men joined her and Costa stood and kissed them all on both cheeks.

"Summer, I'd like to introduce you to my cousins Yasmin and Nick and my uncle Mano. They live in California too," Costa said.

"Oh what part?" Summer stood and shook their hands. "I'm in Northern California. Brentwood Bay."

"No way!" Nick said, giving her a broad smile. "That's where we're from. What are the odds!"

"That's crazy," Yasmin said. "Are you Greek? There are lots of Greek families who emigrated from Lesvos to Brentwood Bay so maybe we're related."

"No," Summer said. "The only link I had to Greece before I came here was that my mom was waitressing in a Greek restaurant when she was pregnant with me."

"So, some time in the nineties?" Nick said. He turned to the older man. "Pop weren't you guys the only Greek restaurant in Brentwood Bay in the nineties?"

"Yes, and still the only good one," his father said, beaming.

"Oh my goodness, maybe she worked for you." Summer's pulse began to quicken. "Her name was Caroline Adams."

Nick and Yasmin turned to their father. "Do you remember a Caroline Adams, Pop?"

The old man's bushy gray eyebrows knitted across his forehead. "In the nineties you say? Your mother will know." He smiled at her and then his face lit up. "Yes, yes, Caroline. She wasn't Greek, but she spoke the language so well. She'd been living here on Lesvos before she came back to the States, I think. One thing I do remember was that she was a very sad person when she came to work for us, but when she left, when she was ready to have her baby, she was so much happier."

Summer's heart squeezed in her chest." Her poor mom. She'd obviously left here under a cloud, but this place must have had a huge impact on her for her to seek out work in a Greek restaurant when she returned.

"Do you remember anything else about her?"

"All that I remember about Caroline is that everyone loved her," Mano said. "I wanted her to meet and marry a Greek boy but she dated a very blond boy, I think."

"That would have been my father. They weren't together very long."

"How is your mother?" Yasmin asked. "Does she still live in Brentwood Bay."

"Summer's mom only recently passed away." Costa's eyes softened as he looked at her..

"She came back for the last couple of months of her life to stay with me in Brentwood Bay," Summer said. "I wish I'd thought to suggest we look you guys up but she was quite sick by then."

"Oh, I'm so sorry," Yasmin said as she touched her arm. "Look, why don't you come over to our table after you've eaten. I'm sure my mom must remember her. We go back to the States tomorrow so we can give you our contact details and you should get in touch when you're home."

"Oh, thank you," Summer said. "I'd love to meet your mom."

Mano, Yasmin and Nick moved away to their table under an enormous tree and Summer and Costa sat back down.

"I can't believe what a coincidence that is?" Summer marveled.

From across the square someone called, "Costa!" A large man by the barbecue was smiling and waving him over.

Costa looked back at Summer. "Excuse me," he said, placing his knife and fork on top of the food. "Will you be okay for a minute? My uncle seems to need me."

"Of course, I will be."

She nodded, and he stood and walked across the square. Her gaze followed him as he strode away, his white shirt, now with the sleeves rolled up, in sharp contrast to his wavy black hair.

For a few moments Summer let her eyes wander, watching people mingle and interact. A couple of men spoke to Costa and at regular intervals slapped him on the back.

An old woman, a black scarf on her head, shuffled toward her and took Costa's chair. As Summer didn't know how to tell her the place was already taken, she just smiled and nodded.

They stared at each other in an uncomfortable silence, and then the old woman grabbed Summer's arm with her leathery hand in a surprisingly firm grip.

"Your mother...Caroline?" The old woman's voice was shaky and coated in such a heavy accent Summer strained to understand. Her thin brows lifted in question, and for a panicked second, Summer wondered if she might be about to suffer another barrage of abuse.

She sat straighter in the chair, her jaw clenched. "Yes," she answered cautiously Should she leave her arm or pull it away? She threw an anxious glance in Costa's direction, silently begging him to turn around. When he didn't, a bullet of dread shot up her spine.

The woman looked around as if to see who was listening, but the others at the table were deep in conversation. "Bad, bad thing," the woman said, squeezing Summer's arm tighter. "Michali, my nephew. Bad, bad thing." And to Summer's distress, the woman began to weep.

Frantically she looked up, but Costa was nowhere to be seen.

The poor woman. Caroline had obviously touched her family in the same way Costa had described. Sadness, tinged with embarrassment, coursed through her body. She carefully took the trembling hand of the woman in her own as something steeled within her.

It was one thing for her mother to teach *her* about dreaming big and living beyond other people's expectations, but that this woman on the other side of the world had been so profoundly affected by her mother's principles was horrifying.

"Michali?" Summer managed to say his name through frozen lips as she rubbed soothing circles on the woman's hand. "Is he gone?"

The old lady wiped her tears with the back of a hand and her dark eyes widened, as if in delight that Summer understood. And then the tears welled again, and she nodded vigorously. "Michali, Maria, Stavros, gone, gone, gone."

A pain burned in Summer's chest. How could she stay here? How could she remain in this village when the memories she ignited caused so much anguish to the people? Her mom would never have intended to do any harm. And hadn't Costa said on the first day she'd met him that much of the village had been in tears when her mother left?

"I'm so sorry," she murmured, and this time she reached out with her free hand to stroke the woman's arm. "I'm sure my mother meant well. Her time in Greece was obviously important to her, and I'm sure she never expected anyone to get hurt. Mom just loved living, and she wanted people to live their best life by being the best version of themselves."

The woman, her brow creasing in question, didn't understand, so Summer stopped speaking. The old lady gently pulled her hand from Summer's and took a white handkerchief with a delicate lace border out of her pocket to dry her cheeks. It was even more heartbreaking for Summer to realize that what was anger once, was now deep-seated sorrow.

As the woman scraped her chair back on the ancient flagstones, Summer squeezed her hand one last time. "I'm so sorry," she said. "Thank you for speaking to me." With a last pat on Summer's arm, the woman turned and walked away.

What a monumental mistake it had been, coming here to retrace the steps of her mother; her peace-loving mother who must have been unaware of the feelings some of the villagers had for her.

She picked up her paper napkin and began twisting it into a rope, and then into a knot. She had to believe her mother didn't know of these feelings. Caroline would never have sent her back here if she had. Would she?

"I'm sorry for leaving you alone so long." Costa pulled his chair out and sat down. "My uncles were teasing me about only spending time with you."

Her heart thudded inside her chest. Had he seen the woman with her?

"Do they know who I am?" The paper napkin shredded and tiny pieces snowed down on the table. Her stomach clenched.

He looked at her, his eyes questioning. "What do you mean?"

Strings of confusion and guilt pulled her stomach tighter. "Like your father, are they wishing you weren't spending time with the daughter of Caroline Adams?"

Thoughts raced—and a lump inched its way from her stomach to her throat. She'd lied when she'd said she didn't mind when people made fun of her mother. She *hated* it. Her mother *loved* people, loved *life*; it tore her apart that there were people harboring ill feelings about her mom so many years on.

"Summer, what do you mean?" A strong, warm hand covered hers, which still gripped what remained of the napkin. The strength that had for so long intimidated her seemed to leach into her skin as his gaze held her steady.

"You have it all wrong. Just because people like my father thought your mother encouraged us to think big, it doesn't mean he hated her."

She couldn't tell him. "I *used* to be *so* proud of her," she managed to say, every cell in her hand, then her arm, then her chest, humming with his touch. "Even when she was making choices about her care, I was heartbroken, but secretly proud, and a little...envious...that she believed in herself so much." Slowly, the tightness in her stomach eased. "There aren't many people who can truly make a difference in the world, but I think Mom believed she was one of those."

And suddenly a thought was born, a thought so frightening she broke her hand free from its warm cocoon.

Had her mother been too scared to return and sell the house? Did she know all along that, when she died, Summer would have to come back here and face the wrath of these villagers?

The scrape of her chair as she thrust it back and stood up was so loud and crude that conversations died around them.

Costa looked up, his face pained with concern. "Summer, what is it?"

"I can't do this anymore." Her hands flapped as she tried to stop the tears coming. "I can't bear to think people hated my mom so much. She was a *good* person...some of her choices might have confused and saddened me sometimes but she had a heart of *gold*. I don't want her to be remembered this way."

She dragged the mauve scarf from the back of the chair and held it to her face. Oh, why had she washed it, scrubbed the scent of her mother out of it forever? "I'm sorry," she said through the gossamer threads to her mom and her memory. "I'm sorry, Costa, I just can't do this anymore."

~

He didn't think twice about going after her. Now he was here —outside her window, hands thrust in his pockets staring at the new pane of glass—Costa wasn't sure what to say. The spring dusk cast orange shadows making the glass flame, and all he wanted was to hold Summer, comfort her...

How could he not tell her the truth now? That her mother was the most influential person in his life, that even though it sounded like a cliché, she had literally made him who he was today. It was inconceivable that Summer had such a distorted view of reality. As much as it pained him, his duty to keep Caroline's secrets was now overridden by his duty to tell Summer the truth. To ease her pain, to help her understand.

He thought about Caroline's last email to him. The only thing she'd stipulated was that he mustn't tell Summer he'd come to ensure the successful sale of the house. She also hadn't forbidden him from saying he'd known her.

He couldn't let Summer go on thinking such terrible things about her mother.

Gently he tapped on the door—once, twice. "Summer, it's Costa. Please let me in."

No movement, no whisper of her tiptoeing across the floor.

He imagined her, lying on crumpled sheets sobbing, and he burned to get to her.

"Summer?"

Her voice came, fluted but firm. "Costa, I'm fine, please go back to the party. I'll see you tomorrow."

"I'm not going anywhere."

"I don't need you anymore, Costa." Pride and self-reliance rang through her words. "I'll never be able to thank you for what you've done for me." But then her voice quivered, and he felt her fragility, bone deep. "But I'd be more comfortable if I could finish this by myself."

His stomach clenched. It wasn't true. She didn't mean it. She *couldn't* mean it.

"Summer, I'm not going anywhere until you understand the truth. You've got completely the wrong idea about your mother's life on the island. It's time you learned about the past."

After a long period of silence, he finally made out the flip-flop of her sandals as she crossed the floor and the click as she lifted the latch.

"You were the one who put this lock on." Her smile was watery. "It's enough to hold back a marauding army."

She stood to the side as he moved through the door, but she was close enough that her warmth soaked into him, as did the scent of jasmine and ocean spray that always seemed to follow her.

The scarf she'd been wearing was nowhere to be seen, and the simplicity of the pink dress and the way her body moved beneath it held his gaze and took his breath away. It was the same way she'd looked when they got married. So beautiful. His wife.

Despite being early dusk, there wasn't much natural light in the house. The electricity still hadn't been connected in this part of the house, and the dancing glow from a row of candles illuminated the ceiling, the bed, her face. The soft curve from her chin to her earlobe seemed iridescent, and he imagined its feather-softness beneath his lips as he marked a line of kisses there.

Summer moved back to the bed and sat cross-legged on the comforter. He pulled the old box over and sat on it, his long legs stretching out in front.

"What happened at the wedding today?" He gently probed.

"I...what do you mean? I met your father...your cousins, some neighbors. You know what happened at the wedding." She stopped and chewed her lip before continuing. "I discovered my mother left a terrible legacy in this place. Something that's been festering for years and I was...I was shocked."

Her voice wavered as she laced her fingers together, and Costa had to jam his hands between his knees to stop himself from going to her. "Why were you shocked?"

~

His question reeled in her mind. Why was he here? What did he want from her? He said he'd come to tell her something, so why was he questioning her?

He sat there as casually as he always did, and she squeezed her fingers tighter. "I was shocked because I didn't realize people would still harbor such strong feelings about someone who left the island so long ago. I also don't understand how people could have got my mom so wrong. Yes, she was forward-thinking. Yes, she was passionate and broad-minded, but..." She swallowed hard.

He leaned forward, eyes widening. "My father is not *everyone* in this village," he said quietly. "Just because he had expectations for his son that weren't met, doesn't mean everyone in the village felt that way." He smiled then, the most heart-melting genuine smile she'd ever seen and her whole body softened.

"Your mother was an *inspiration* here."

He pulled the box closer, the tips of his designer boots almost touching the edge of her bed. "She came at a time when people really needed to learn English, so that when they traveled from the island for work, as many of them had to, they were prepared."

119

"So, you're saying her teaching English benefited the children here?"

"Of course." His eyes sparked. "But it wasn't only that. She gave us a fresh way of looking at ourselves, at the world, and made us understand that even though we came from this tiny island, we could all be whatever we wanted and live our dreams."

With sparkling clarity, Summer realized Costa was speaking about himself. "Is that the way it was for you?"

He tapped a fist on his forehead, as if judging how far to go with his explanation, then his face broke into a broad, heartwarming smile. "I owe your mother everything, Summer. If it wasn't for her, I would've stayed on the island, doing the only thing expected of me and what my family had been doing for generations, and it would have killed me." He paused for breath. "I'm not saying that a life here wouldn't be amazing for others. I've got cousins who have built incredible businesses and who have beautiful families. So many people love island life. But it wasn't for me, and your mother showed me that."

"Which is the reason you offered to marry me to help with the renovation." She paused. "Because I wasn't such a stranger."

His eyes dropped and the confidence she'd seen a moment ago seemed to dampen. "Yes."

The clenching in Summer's stomach gave way to a warmth that spread outward and upward to her chest, her arms, her face. Someone in this village had respected her mother, *did* understand the real Caroline. That it was Costa was that much sweeter.

He looked up at her once more, his infinite gaze holding her still. "You should be *so* proud of the way she taught us about making good choices for ourselves, but always with the background of what was good for society. She taught us that money was the least important thing in the world—that if you were following your heart, what you loved and had a passion for, you'd be the richest person you could be."

The image of the old woman sprang to Summer's mind and for a moment the warm feeling cooled. She wouldn't tell him about the encounter—how could she? It was obvious from the passion in his voice, the way he spoke with such force, that he truly believed what he was saying.

"If I'm honest, it saddened me the way you spoke about your mom when you first arrived," he said. "I wanted you to understand what a wonderful, influential, amazing person she was."

A chord of energy pulsed between them, his gaze holding her mesmerized. Close without touching, it was as heavenly as it was tortuous.

She could taste her need for his lips on hers as desire smoldered in the depths of his eyes.

"Thank you." Her words were thick with want. A warm, low pulse deep within her body radiated outward.

"What for?" His voice was low, his gaze never leaving hers.

Now. She needed to feel his skin on hers. The beat became harder, faster, a rhythm of desire so strong it had the power to overwhelm her, and she had to say the words in a rush while she still made sense. "For caring so much."

He stood then and moved, now just inches from the bed, heat radiating from him. She longed for his kisses to scorch her skin.

In one swift movement, he pulled her toward him so she kneeled on the bed—at the same level, but only inches from his mouth.

"How could I not care?" he whispered as he reached for her face, and with both hands gently drew her to him so his mouth finally met hers.

His breath, at first warm and sweet with wine, danced across her mouth, the touch of his lips on hers an exhilarating shock that sent pulses through her body as it cried out for more. She slid both hands up the back of his neck until her fingers buried themselves in his thick, ebony hair.

Harder, stronger, blinded by desire, she wanted all of him now, needed to feel the completeness that only knowing his entire body would give. She had to feel the release only he could provide.

Gently, he pushed her back on the bed, and as she wriggled, her dress rode up. Carefully, he placed his hand on her calf and slid it, inch by excruciating inch, up her trembling leg until his fingers caressed the hem of her dress, all the while holding her gaze.

"I've wanted you from the moment I saw you," he said thickly as his hands caressed her quivering stomach. Then he pulled her close, and her overwhelming desire for him plunged her into a world she'd only ever hoped for.

The taste of him was sublime, his lips soft and demanding, playful and asking a lone question. The feel of him as her hands smoothed the skin of his throat, moving across the rigid mound of his Adam's apple filled her with the desire for more.

As she tugged his white shirt from the confines of his pants and felt the hard pulse of his abdomen under her fingertips, Summer wanted the whole of him. She wanted the entire package, his body and his mind, and tonight she was going to have it all.

Something woke her. Was it the swallows? When something moved beside her, she realized with a start what it was. She was in bed. With Costa.

Was it midnight? Dawn? The candles were out, and she couldn't see her hand in front of her face.

For a second she lay rigid, recalling the incredible events of hours ago. How could it have happened? How could she, Summer Adams, have ended up in bed with someone like Costa Nicoliedies? Someone so confident, so magnetic. But the memory of his lovemaking sent a ripple through her as she remembered his tenderness, his generosity.

Confused at her tangle of emotions, she tried to will herself back to sleep, but she desperately needed the bathroom. It was so snug under the covers with heat radiating from the magnificent length of Costa's body, she wanted to snuggle back down and drink in his warmth.

Carefully, she inched her way to the side of the bed. With searching fingers, she found her bathrobe and tied it firmly around her waist.

Her palms flat on the ground, she felt for her phone and sighed with relief as her fingers closed around its case. She swiped down for the light, stepped onto the floor, and her foot slid on something.

The real estate magazine.

She flicked the beam down to move it out of her way...and her heart stilled.

The photograph.

Her mother. Her mother and her nameless, long-forgotten lover.

Heart thudding, she bent down and picked it up, the phone light causing the image to come into sharp focus.

The woman in the photo might have longer hair, but the young man with black hair, the smile, the long languid look and the passion burning between them? This photo could've been taken in this very room now—not thirty years ago. She slammed the image to her chest. What had she done?

Slowly, she pulled the photo away and once more shone

the light on it, profound sadness and horror forming a bitter cocktail inside her.

History had repeated itself. In one crazy, ironic second, Summer realized what had happened here.

I've become my mother.

In one random moment, the thrill of being Costa's wife had carried her away. Making love with him as if it was something they could do anytime, anywhere. But this wasn't real. What she had with Costa was what her mother had had with the man in this photo all those years ago. Just like her mother, she was proving she could flit from one place to the next, leaving only sadness in her wake.

As if blinded, she groped her way to the bathroom, her heart racing. In one hand she clutched the photo, in the other her phone. Why had she done it? Why had she allowed herself to do exactly what she'd criticized her mother for? Was she looking for some crazy way to get closer to her memory?

Reaching the bathroom, she wished she could shut the door. Instead, she sat on the icy floor with trembling fingers, and heart thumping, she directed the light onto the picture.

Temporary. That's all her mother had wanted things in her life to be. From the nameless young man in the photo, to her stints all around the world, to her failure in long-term relationships with men. Even her hold on money had been fleeting. Yes, maybe all those things had been for honorable reasons, but the fact remained that nothing with her mother had lasted.

Her heart galloped as she realized with sickening clarity that what she'd just had with Costa could only ever be that— temporary. He moved between cities on the opposite side of the world to her, and he celebrated the fact that he could avoid community and stability.

A wave of profound sadness broke over her as feelings she'd kept suffocated for days fought their way to the surface.

Hot tears pushed at the corner of her eyes. Costa was special—he made her feel grounded, as if suddenly she truly belonged somewhere, with someone. But it was all an illusion, all so impossible, just like the piece of paper they'd signed. All so...temporary.

She sat a little straighter, the hard wall pressing into her back as she screwed her eyes tight to banish the tears.

I will not live that way.

She had a reliable job to return home to, "Safe Anchorage" to close on. This threat of impermanence wasn't going to manifest. It had to stop right here. Right now.

Movement from the room next door made her snap the light on her phone off.

"Summer?"

She held her breath.

There was a thump as his feet hit the floor. "Summer, are you okay?"

She couldn't hide, couldn't pretend she was someone else. Pretend they wanted the same things in life. Now was the time to say it, get her thoughts out in the open and forget about the whole, complicated mess.

"I'm okay," she called, commanding her voice not to betray her. "I'll be back in a minute. Can you light a candle?"

By the time she returned to him, light was once more dancing across the ceiling. Costa was sitting up in bed with the covers mercifully pulled over his stomach.

Clutching her robe tighter, she sat on the side of the bed.

The shadows cast by the candles made him even more gorgeous; his eyes darker, cheekbones more defined, the coffee color of his skin deeper.

Remember the photo, remember the photo.

"Costa," she began, keeping her eyes away from the tug of his body, "we've made a mistake."

He said nothing, his gaze not moving from hers.

"We got carried away with the pretense we've created here. I'm here for a short time...you're here for a short time. We both have jobs to do."

If he'd just nod his head, say something in agreement, this wouldn't be so excruciating.

"I appreciate everything you've done for me, but I don't want to leave this village with the same bad feelings that followed my mother."

Why couldn't he just stop looking so relaxed and wonderful and gorgeous? She dug her nails into her palms to stop herself from falling into him. "I hope you understand."

He opened his mouth—those lips that had devoured her, whispered to her—as if to say something, but then he closed it again.

Was she crazy? What harm could a holiday fling with someone so thoughtful and caring do?

A lifetime of following someone else's dreams—and she couldn't risk it.

"I'm sorry you feel that way."

She swallowed at the intensity and power of his voice and at how different they were.

He reached for his suit trousers, turned away and while still seated, put them on. She stared at his back, so brown and broad, and chewed her lip at the thought she wouldn't caress it again.

Finally, he turned back, his bare chest taunting her until he dragged on his shirt.

He tugged his boots on, and when he was fully clothed, he moved around to her side of the bed and pulled her up, her body melting into him.

"You are beautiful, Summer Adams. I'm not sorry I made

love to you, and I'll do it again when you realize we are not a mistake."

She swallowed as she looked up into his impossibly dark eyes.

"Tomorrow I will still be here to help you as I always have, and I will not touch you if that's what you want, but I will make you see, make you see clearly, that you are wrong."

CHAPTER NINE

*S*ummer dreamed her heart had turned to iron. It looked the same, with all its pipes and chambers, but it was cold and metallic. When it beat inside her chest, it hit hard against her ribs and sounded like a hammer on a bell.

As she swam up from the depths of sleep the noise continued, "tonk, tonk, tonk," and she clutched wildly at her chest with both hands, expecting the cutting edge of metal.

When the noise didn't stop, she sat up and slowly realized it was coming from the back of the house.

Pulling on her robe, she tiptoed through to the bathroom. From the way the sun painted the opposite wall, it must be past eight. It wasn't surprising she'd slept late; she'd still been awake when dawn broke, reliving her moments with Costa. Thinking of him lying alone in the basement. At least, she assumed he was still here, as she hadn't heard him leave last night.

Still the "tonk, tonk" continued, and when she opened the newly glazed window, she saw Takis and Costa bending over a pipe coming from the side of the house.

The moment Costa looked up, the confused tangle of emotions inside her twisted tighter. She wanted to suffocate the warnings in her head and just go to him, feel his solid body and bury her doubts.

"Good morning," he said, his eyes not darting away in embarrassment but carefully holding her fragile stare.

"*Kalimera*." Clutching the robe, she nodded to Takis then Costa.

"Takis is fixing some leaking pipes Socrates found yesterday. They need to be done before he finishes the plastering downstairs, and before you complete the kitchen."

Her ears accepted the words, but her brain wouldn't process them as her insides turned molten, her gaze frozen—cruel reminders of the effect he had on her.

He acted like nothing had changed—that he hadn't kissed her throat so tenderly she'd whispered his name. That she hadn't clung to him, their hearts merging as he'd pulled her closer.

"Thanks," she managed. "I'll just get dressed. Have you heard the *koulouri* man?"

Costa pointed to a paper bag sitting on a rock. "Petro went by hours ago. It's ten o'clock."

He could've teased her, made a sarcastic comment about having a late night, but he didn't.

Of course he didn't.

She went through the motions of getting dressed and eating an orange for breakfast. Were her actions last night unjustified? Costa wasn't responsible for what his father or the old woman had said. Why was it necessary to put such a dramatic halt to things?

She couldn't stop thinking about him, couldn't stop the quickening of her heartbeat when she remembered him pulling her closer last night. Closing her eyes tight, she tried to block the memory of the way he'd said her name, his voice

129

raw with need. The firm planes of his muscles pressed to her body. But the more she tried to ignore the memories, the stronger her feelings became.

I want more.

She shook her head and opened her eyes. The truth was too clear.

Losing sight of her dreams—her own home, her own security—wasn't an option. The two things she'd never had, the two things she craved. Costa had said he never stayed in one place for long, that he wouldn't want to be tied down, didn't have time for a relationship as well as work. All they could ever have was something temporary.

And it wasn't enough.

Her mother was the perfect example of how casual relationships added nothing to security and stability in your life. No wonder he'd admired her so much. Costa and Caroline had shared the same values.

All she had to do was get through the next two weeks without imagining or remembering, and then she'd be home free.

The tapping noise at the back of the house stopped, and a moment later Costa appeared holding the paper bag.

"Coffee break?"

"I've only just had breakfast." If she could keep busy, doing things in different rooms, working away from him, it would be much easier.

"Do I need to go to the *kafenion* instead?" His eyebrows raised, telling her it was okay to be friendly, she didn't need to freeze him out.

She still needed his help. "Of course not. I'll make you one."

"You really need some chairs," Costa said as he went to sit on the box. "You'll have a kitchen soon and it would be nice to have a table and chairs. You'll have room when we finish fixing the hole in the bedroom wall and move your bed in there."

Summer put water, sugar and coffee in the small pot with the long handle the way she'd seen him do it, concentrating hard on her actions so she didn't have to look at him. "I don't need chairs in here to sell the place. A working kitchen will be fine." She flinched at her cool tone. She didn't want to seem cold but needed to get their relationship back on a professional footing.

Turning on the gas, she flicked the flame then placed the coffeepot on top of the ring. "How long does this need to boil?" The slightest shake in her hands made the cups and saucers chatter as she placed them on the bench.

"There's a bit of an art to it. I'll show you."

He came and stood beside her, the bright red T-shirt he wore drawing her eyes to his rock hard abs, the place she'd stroked, the place where... Her eyes snapped back to the pot.

"See it simmer—the little bubbles it creates at the side?" he asked. "As soon as the volume moves up the side of the pot, you take it off the heat. Just a minute more should do it."

They stood in silence, staring at the ridiculous pot, an unspoken energy heating the air between them.

Finally, the froth began moving up the side. "Now, take it off the heat," he said, and when she did, "**and** as soon as it goes down you put it back on again."

She did as he said.

"You do that three times and then you'll have a perfect froth on the top of the coffee when you pour it into the cups." He moved back to the box. "We call the froth *filakia*. Little kisses."

As she sucked in a breath, the pot seemed to hang in midair. Was he teasing her?

She put it back on the heat and, while still concentrating

on the pot, blew out a tight breath. "**Costa,** I'm sorry about last night."

"I know, you said." His voice held the usual confidence, no judgment, just strength.

"I hope it hasn't changed things between us." She spoke slowly and carefully, but with as little emotion as she could.

"Of course it's changed things between us."

Feelings and words warred inside her in a mass of contradiction. Summoning strength, she pushed the feelings away and let the words have their freedom. "Then I hope it won't get in the way of us working together." She pulled the pot off the flame for the last time and carefully poured the coffee, kisses and all, into the cups.

Carefully passing the cup to him, she stayed focused on the moving liquid, trying not to spill it. When he didn't take the saucer, it forced her to look into those deep, dark eyes as he smiled, and her heartbeat skidded to a halt.

Costa slapped the plaster on the old gray wall harder than was necessary. It was calming—moving the trowel backward and forward to smooth the surface—but it was really just a cover for the misshapen wall beneath, a little like the face he wanted to present to Summer.

Even though she wanted to make light of what had happened between them, he was determined she shouldn't be regretful. The intensity, the passion, with which she'd made love was evidence enough that she didn't see it as a mistake. She was just being careful, protecting herself.

If he was honest with himself, the power of his feelings had taken him by surprise last night. There was no question she was beautiful and vulnerable and infuriatingly independent—but it was her determination to succeed, to live her dream, that truly drew him to her. That, at least, was something they had in common.

The force with which she'd cut the night short had taken him completely by surprise. He wasn't used to it. *He* was the one who called a halt to things—when women got too close, asked for money or status—it was a surefire method of self-protection. So why had he been so slow with Summer? Because she hadn't asked him for anything, except for help with the house, and *that* he'd freely offered.

Stronger feelings—the pull of desire and the hunger of need began to surface—but he pushed them back down. It would happen—it always did—when she realized how much money he had it would change things between them, but by then their marriage would be dissolved and she'd no longer need him.

He bent to collect another scoop of plaster when a scream, cut off by an enormous thud, turned his blood frigid.

Summer.

He took the basement steps two at a time, the sickening silence ringing in his ears.

He emerged into the light and saw her lying awkwardly on the hard ground. His throat and chest tightened in terror. The old wooden ladder lay next to her, one of its rungs sticking out at an angle like a wayward tooth.

"Summer?" He knelt by her side. Her eyes were shut, her face frighteningly pale.

He yelled for Takis, then reached out a shaking hand and touched her neck. Her gentle pulse played against his fingers and he let out the breath he didn't know he was holding.

"Takis?" he shouted again, the catch in his voice taking him by surprise. Then he remembered his cousin had gone to the square to get some supplies.

He had to get her to the medical center—fast—but he

couldn't get his father's car down the cobbled path in this part of the village.

Guilt clutched his stomach. She'd asked him to help with the swallows, but he'd dismissed it as unnecessary.

Summer let out a small moan and he moved his face closer to hers. Carefully, he smoothed her hair and to his horror felt the sticky ooze of blood.

Panicked, and without thought for damaged limbs, he cradled her to his chest and a small crease settled on her brow as if she were in pain.

He wouldn't allow anything to happen to her. He'd get helicopters, specialists from the mainland if necessary. The constriction in his throat closed further.

He momentarily marveled at how light she was. That someone with so much strength and presence should be so delicate scared him. He placed a lingering kiss on her forehead, hoping to imprint his strength into her.

He hurried up the hill to the doctor's house, silently begging for Summer to be okay. To have her luminous blue eyes open and trained on him, her hand reaching for his. To look at him like she did last night in wonder, her shy smile heating his blood. This was his fault. What price was his loyalty to Caroline? He'd been pig-headed, blinded by his desire to meet his teacher's last wishes. He could have come back, met Summer, paid for the renovations so she could sell the house, and nobody would have been any the wiser.

Thoughts banged and bounced in his brain as he strode faster up the hill, stopping every few feet to check the fluttery pulse in her neck.

If he'd come back and used his money like he usually did, there would have been no time for soul-searching, no empty moments to question what he was doing with his life. He wouldn't have experienced the simple acts of renovating a house, installing glass, manual labor surrounded by people he cared about and who cared about him. If he'd just paid for everything, he wouldn't have had to spend every day with Summer, they wouldn't have had to get married and he wouldn't have fallen...

His head jerked away from her ghostly face as the power of his thoughts savaged his body, and he stumbled on the cobbles. At the same time, a young woman came out of her house asking what was wrong, and he begged her to run to the doctor's house.

His thighs burning from the effort, Costa willed himself forward. He would let nothing happen to Summer. He'd tell her the truth. All of it.

For a second, Summer thought it was the same dream, only this time it wasn't only her heart made of metal, but her skull too. As she opened her lids just a fraction, the pain of the light caused her to squeeze them shut again. Had Takis stopped working on the pipes and moved his hammer to her head?

The nest. In her mind's eye she could see it—all rough twigs and plaited feathers—and then her body stretching and stretching until finally her fingertips scraped closer and she'd managed to drag it toward her. Had there been something in it? She couldn't remember, but she'd had a sense of urgency to work quickly before the swallows returned. She remembered having a hold on it, the outside coarse and spiky but soft and smooth on the inside.

"Summer?"

It was Costa's voice. But why was he calling her from the end of a tunnel, each syllable moving in and out of her hearing, round and hollow?

Something held her hand. Another piece of metal? No, this was warm and strong and had a heartbeat all of its own.

"Summer, can you hear me?"

It was too draining to reply, and anyway, Costa wasn't part of her heart anymore. She couldn't remember why, but the thought of him made the hammering in her head louder and a shroud of regret hugged her soul tight as she fell back into an exhausted sleep.

What felt like much later, the sound of low voices speaking Greek roused her, and when she opened her eyes the pain wasn't so sharp—just a mighty throb.

She was lying slightly propped up and needed no translation to know she was in hospital. Her brain ached as she tried to remember what had happened, why she might be here, but still all she could remember was the rough and smooth feel of the nest.

"Summer, you're awake."

The two men who'd been talking moved to her bedside, but she didn't recognize either of them. They were both young and serious looking. Had she lost her memory? Her heart raced.

"My name is Dr Petrakis, I'm your neurosurgeon, and this is Dr Ilias, your orthopedic surgeon."

Two surgeons? Her heart beat faster, matching the pounding in her head. How ill was she? Where was she? What happened? Certainly not in a small island hospital if she had two specialists attending her.

"Where am I?" she asked, hoping it didn't sound as desperate as she felt.

The neurosurgeon moved closer and flicked a thin torch in front of her eyes. "Do you know your name? he asked.

"Summer Adams."

"And where are you from?" His tone was grave.

"Brentwood Bay in California."

He stood back and switched off the penlight. "Then why don't you know where you are?"

Summer had to think hard, which hurt her brain. Was this a riddle? "I just assumed I wasn't in the village if I had two specialists looking after me. Unless you've moved me to a bigger town."

The two men exchanged glances then the orthopedic surgeon said, "You are still on Lesvos, Ms Adams. In the main hospital."

If she were still on Lesvos and had two specialists looking after her, it could only mean one thing—a massive hospital bill. She closed her eyes at the sickening thought. Why hadn't she been more careful? She'd taken all the precautions to stop her asthma flaring up, never thinking of something like this. She only had the most basic insurance cover that most definitely wouldn't pay for a lengthy hospital stay.

"Have you operated?" she gasped, realizing her foot was in plaster.

"We've done what we needed to do." Dr Ilias smiled at her. "You had a nasty fall. You were unconscious for quite some time, resulting in significant concussion which is now improving, and you've broken a bone in your ankle."

She gazed around the room. "How did I get here? I don't remember."

"A friend brought you. He's been here most of the time you've been unconscious. I believe he'll return later."

"But I can't... How long will I need to be here?" The thought of the medical bill climbing every day made her nauseous. Perhaps if she could get some crutches...?

"You'll stay another four to five days as the progress of your brain injury is observed, and if all is well and you're mobile, you'll be permitted to return home."

Home. The realization hit her as a gut punch. How was she going to complete the renovation now? There were only two weeks left before she had to be back at work and to close on "Safe Anchorage". And even if she could finish in time, an enormous chunk of the profit would now need to go on her hospital bill.

Nausea swirled in her sickening stomach.

"We'll leave you now," one of the surgeons said. "The local doctor can take care of you from here. We wish you well." And with that they were gone.

Summer looked out the small window and across the bay. Puffy clouds hugged a sapphire sky. Small boats bobbed and a large cruise liner inched its way into the port. It felt as if each cog in her brain needed to engage individually before she could form a rational thought.

It was over—time to accept defeat. As soon as she was able, she'd get a ticket on a ferry and head back to Athens. And what would she leave behind? A past that could not be put right.

Tears burned her throat and threatened to escape her eyes.

Perhaps if she donated the house back to the community, it would make up for what her mother had taken away from the place. Then she'd have to come up with the money to pay Costa for his four weeks' work. Rubbing her hands across her face, she drew a long breath. If she couldn't put things right, there was absolutely no point in staying.

"Hi."

The hairs on the back of her neck rose, and pulling her hands away from her face, she forced a smile as Costa entered the room. Again, she tried to remember why she had such a sad feeling when she looked at him, even though every thread in her physical body pulled toward him. His red T-shirt had white stripes of plaster smeared across the front that matched a smudge on his cheek.

"I'm sorry I wasn't here when you woke," he said, smiling as he leaned in to kiss her.

As if struck by lightning, Summer's head snapped back, causing pain to ricochet through her skull. There *was* something wrong. He mustn't kiss her, mustn't get close. Goose bumps cascaded down her arms, and she shoved them under the covers as Costa pulled away.

"How are you feeling?" He drew up a chair, a small frown touching his brow.

She had to concentrate hard to form a sentence. "As if a little man has taken up residence in my skull and is doing some renovations." She'd be positive, cheery, as if all her dreams for her future and her own home hadn't ended.

"I've just seen your doctors. They think you'll start feeling better in a couple of days and can perhaps get out of bed by the end of the week."

"Do you know when the local doctor will come by?" Summer asked. "I'd really like to get up sooner." The thought of the doctor's bill flashed red in her head.

"I...Would you like a glass of water?" He busied himself with the jug and glass beside the bed.

She worried the sheet. "Do you think you could talk to them for me...soon?"

"They've gone." He handed her the glass. She sipped the cold water, which relieved her parched throat.

"Gone where?" She placed the glass on the bedside table.

"Back to Athens. They're from a hospital in Athens."

Shocked, she could only stare at him. "And they came here to see me? How did they get here so quickly?" she finally managed.

Costa shrugged, then walked over to the window. "You needn't worry."

She tried to sit up straighter, but the second she moved, pain zapped through her head and leg.

"But I can't afford—"

"They're friends of mine, Summer. You don't need to worry. I called in a favor."

"A favor?"

His back was still turned. "They're both from the island so it's good for them to come back to see what's going on at the hospital here."

Had he paid for them to come? It must have cost a fortune. One thing was for sure; he wouldn't give her a straight answer. She wouldn't push it. For now.

"So what happened? I don't remember."

He turned away from the window, his face relaxing. He moved back to the bed and sat in the chair. "I'm not exactly sure. I was doing some plastering downstairs and heard a crash. It looked like you'd been doing something up the ladder and slipped—a rung was broken."

"The nest," she said slowly. "I remember lifting a tile off the roof and seeing the nest there, just out of reach. I must have leaned in too far and..." A terrible thought gripped her. "Did you see the nest? The birds?"

"No, I didn't." His smile was warm and concerned. "But then again, I had other things to think about."

"Thank you." Why were her thoughts such a mess of contradiction? "Do you think you could go back and check for me? Imagine if they're all ready to lay eggs and they go back to find the nest gone. Would you look?"

"Of course I will. That is, if I'm still welcome." His smile deepened; a sexy smile she'd seen when.... The skin on her face slackened as she remembered what had happened the night before the accident. Thinking about it made her brain spin all the more. They'd made love, long passionate love, and then she'd...basically told him to leave.

Why was he still here?

"Well, I guess this is it." She dug her nails into her palm, as if to suffocate the truth. "There's no way I'm going to get the house finished and sold in two weeks if I'm hobbling around on one foot."

"Of course you can still finish," Costa said, the sexy smile staying put. "Nothing's changed. I can still do the work with the boys. You can carry on giving lessons to Socrates and Athina. We'll just make sure someone else does the ladder work this time."

"But the expense of me in here. I don't have adequate insurance and—"

"That means you're going to need the money from the house sale even more. If we're one person down, it means you'll need to give more lessons so Socrates and Takis can finish quicker and we can organize that sale."

He was right. Where else was she going to get the money for hospital bills from—not to mention the expense of the specialists? Now more than ever she needed to get this wretched house sold, and quickly.

And then she remembered. Hope bloomed in her tired brain. *The ring.*

"Costa, I need you to get me something."

"Sure. Clothes? Toothbrush? You name it."

"Yes, please. Just some things to get me through the next few days, but there's something else too." How she wished she could do this herself. "In the box—you know the one we found up in the attic—there's a gold ring in there."

He nodded.

"I need you to sell it for me."

He shifted in his chair. "Are you sure? Don't you think the ring might have belonged to your mother?"

"Of course it belonged to my mother." Fingers of guilt crept their way through her chest.

"Then wouldn't it be nice to keep it—as a memento?"

Summer tried to turn to him to emphasize how important this was to her, but again pain shot through her leg to the rest of her body. She groaned and fell back. "If I thought it was important to her, I would never dream of selling it. But it wasn't. She left it here, probably with the intention of never returning. It obviously meant nothing."

His eyes narrowed.

"I've got this," she said, pulling the *tiki* out from beneath her hospital gown. "This meant everything to her. She always wore it, and it means more to me than a ring that was never meant to be found."

"You'll probably only get a couple of hundred Euros for it."

"A couple of hundred seems like a fortune right now. Please, Costa. It'll mean I've got some breathing space. Please do this for me."

Costa let himself into Summer's house and went straight to the box on the floor. She was probably right. The ring mustn't have been important to Caroline or she wouldn't have left it behind, but it still seemed a shame to sell something that might have belonged to her mom.

He pulled out a small piece of material and unwrapped it, his large fingers fumbling with the tiny parcel, and the gold ring fell to the floor.

Picking it up, he marveled at how shiny it was. Nearly thirty years in the box and it still looked new. It was very small, so clearly made to fit a woman's finger. Turning it over he noticed writing on the inside of the band and looked more closely. Με όλη μου την αγάπη. Πάντα.

All of my love. Always.

So, someone had given the ring to Caroline and she'd left it here. He must ask his father who the man–M—in the photo with Caroline might have been. Maybe he had given it to her? And if he had, what had become of him?

What the hell was he going to do?

Summer was in pain, in a hospital, with no money, and still the enormous task of getting this house ready in front of her. What did he know about not having any money, living day-to-day with the threat of everything crumbling around his ears?

He put the ring in his pocket, closed the box and walked out into the late afternoon sun. He'd been lucky that, technically, getting the doctors from Athens hadn't cost him anything. They'd both benefited from scholarships he'd set up when they were in medical school and were more than happy to help him out. But what about this ring? She'd ask him if he'd sold it and what would he tell her? Until he unearthed the story behind it, he wasn't going to sell it.

The image of her lying in the hospital bed kept playing in his mind. Her face pale, pain crossing her features in moments she didn't think he was looking. He'd wanted to touch her, hold her, kiss the scar on her delicate cheek. But he hadn't. She'd pulled away and her words from the night before came between them.

It was a mistake.

He walked around the side of the house to where the accident happened and saw the ladder leaning like a drunk against the wall of the house. He'd repair the rung as soon as possible to avoid any further accidents. Not that Summer would be using a ladder anytime soon.

As he turned to go, something caught his eye. In a small hollow, at the edge of the bank, lay the discarded bird's nest, and he bent to pick it up. Was Summer right? If he were to put it back, would they come home? Or would the touch of humans taint it? Looking closer, he noticed a damp patch at the edge and then looked back at the ground where it had lain.

The shell of an egg, smashed, lay on the ground, a dribble of yolk staining the earth beside it.

The next afternoon, Summer finished texting Bella and Frances, two friends from work and changed position for what seemed like the hundredth time. Although the view from her bed was breathtaking, and the nurse who came in friendly, there was only one person she'd been waiting for all day.

She'd had the dream again last night, about turning metallic, only this time her house had transformed itself. Instead of glass and plaster, the walls had become the iron bars of a birdcage she shared with the swallows. A prison for a home.

A lovely nurse who spoke very little English had noticed Summer's boredom levels and had brought in a pile of magazines—Greek magazines. They'd sat there most of the morning, but now she'd checked all her emails and was desperate enough to pick one up and flick through it. It was similar to women's magazines she read when waiting for the dentist—lots of red carpet shots, fashion advice and headlines with exclamation points.

While she hadn't asked about the cost of her hospital stay, she was hoping Costa would come by today with the money from selling the ring. That it was now late in the afternoon and he hadn't shown his face made her think he might be trying to avoid her. He'd seemed anxious to keep working on the house and was probably spending the day doing that.

Was he thinking about her as he went about his work?

She squeezed her eyes shut and battled another vision of

him reaching for her, touching her with a look of desire. Her eyes snapped open as she tried to stop her body's response to her thoughts, but little rivers of pleasure flooded her bloodstream as she remembered his lips on her neck, *her* lips kissing a trail over his stomach.

She put down the first magazine and picked up the next. On the cover was a beautiful woman posing in front of a line of paparazzi. There were also smaller inset photos of couples at the same event. One of a stunning man in an ebony suit. Summer held the magazine closer and her heart raced.

There was no question. It was Costa.

CHAPTER TEN

*I*n the photo, Costa wore a tuxedo with a white scarf draping the lapels. On his arm was one of the most beautiful women Summer had ever seen, her cerise gown making a bold contrast with the jet-black hair washing her shoulders.

For a moment she let the magazine drop. She had a head injury, that was all. How many Greek men were there with midnight black hair and unforgettable faces? Probably hundreds of thousands. And he didn't live in Greece anyway, at least that's what he'd said.

Slowly she picked up the magazine. If only she could read the caption. She thought she could make out which words were names; one began with what looked like a K but was much longer than "Costa". She reached for the bell. It was crazy, but she had to know.

Thoughts careened into each other as she tried to work out how she felt. Was the woman a girlfriend? A lover?

As she waited for the nurse, she impatiently flicked to the next page. There he was again, with *another* woman. This time a very busty blonde, and they were on the deck of a sleek boat.

Slowly, confusion slid into hurt, and then a rock of shame lodged firmly in her throat. Of course, he had another life; he'd told her that.

And why wouldn't he have women lining up—he was gorgeous. When their marriage was dissolved, he'd be free to go back to his life. He didn't owe her an explanation of who he was, and she had asked little beyond where he lived and how long he'd been away from the island. These pictures suggested he was much more than a translator.

Thank goodness she'd called a halt to things when she did. She'd never compete with these women, and if he weren't stuck here helping her...

"*Neh?*" A young nurse she'd never seen before stood at the door, holding a tray and smiling.

Summer beckoned her in, at the same time feeling guilty for wasting her time. *Please let her speak English.*

"This man," she said, pointing at the first photograph and then the second.

Just as she'd seen with Athina, the young nurse's eyes widened. "Ah, Costa Nicoliedies. He is so handsome. Every Greek girl *loves* him."

The women in the magazine looked as though they did.

"He is very famous," the nurse continued, "and one of the richest Greeks in the world. He comes from here. From Lesvos. I've heard that he's back in his village for the summer, but I have not seen him yet." She took the magazine from Summer and looked closer. "Here he is with Katarina Moutsi. She is a famous actress in our country. And this one is Alexia Tavros. She is a Victoria Secrets model."

"Oh." Summer looked down at her beaten body, bruised limbs sticking out of the hospital gown, and suddenly felt extremely self-conscious. "Which word says Costa there?"

The nurse pointed to the word beginning with K. "Costa is short for Konstantinos."

Her stomach dropped. Without a doubt, it was him.

She should've known from their very first meeting that there was something different about him—the reaction of the people in the coffee shop, his reserved air.

How could she have thought he'd be interested in *her*? And why on earth would he spend time with her when he was used to walking down red carpets and lounging around on super yachts?

"Thank you," she whispered to the nurse who still gazed at the photos. The girl nodded and smiled before handing the magazine back, picking up her tray and leaving the room.

The minute she was gone, Summer threw back the rest of the bedclothes. The walls were closing in. It was mortifying that she'd had to ask for Costa's help; that he'd done it all without payment. Then she remembered what she'd asked him to do with the ring and cringed. He must think her pathetic.

Gingerly, she moved her good leg over the side of the bed, then with both hands she dragged the one in the plaster cast down too. The sooner she was up and around and independent again, the better. As soon as the house was finished, she could leave.

A chair sat to the side of the bed, and she hooked her good leg around the frame and dragged it toward her.

Taking a deep breath, she slid down the edge of the bed until both feet were on the floor. If she could get her balance, get upright for a start, she'd be on her way. Pulling her head up, the room suddenly spun—walls merged into floors, curtains into cabinets. Squeezing her eyes shut, she took another breath.

"Is that such a good idea?"

Of course he had to arrive right at that moment. Nausea squeezed her belly, causing her to shut her eyes tighter.

"Here, let me help."

In a second, his sure, warm hands held her shoulders and steadied her. Slowly, she opened her eyes to the black expanse of his T-shirt hugging his chest. When she drew another breath, his warm, musk scent calmed and relaxed her and as quickly as it had come, the nausea was gone.

In one swift movement, he picked her up and laid her gently back on the bed.

"Did the nurse say it was okay to get out of bed? She said she'd just been in here when she stopped to talk to me."

Partly because the room was still moving, but mostly because she didn't want to look at him, Summer closed her eyes.

"No." She sighed.

"You were impatient."

"Something like that."

He continued talking, but she couldn't register the words. The magazine was only inches from his hand.

Maybe if she turned over it would slide to the floor and he wouldn't notice. She jerked her good knee, and the magazine slithered.

Costa grabbed it before it fell. "No wonder you were trying to get out of bed. You must be bored if all you've got to read are gossip magazines in a language you don't understand."

He tossed it onto the bedside table, and Summer breathed a sigh of relief.

"I've been helping Takis get the kitchen ready," he said. "There wasn't a lot to do, and when you have a minute, you can choose the cooker and bench top you want him to put in."

She was silent.

"From a catalogue. I'll bring you a catalogue."

"Sure, that would be great." All she could think about was the actress, the model—were they girlfriends? Dates? And why did she care, anyway? The photo of her mother and the young man on the beach slid into her mind. No doubt their relationship began and ended just as hers had that night with Costa. "Did you find the ring?

He held her gaze. "Yes, I did."

She waited.

Silence stretched between them.

"Did you take it to the jeweler?"

"Yes, I did," he said again. "And you don't need to worry about your hospital bill. There is still a small amount outstanding, but they're happy to receive that before you leave the country."

Well, that was surprising, about the ring. From the way he'd always talked of her mother and the way he seemed to value things from the past, as well as with what she knew of his attitude to money, she'd expected him to refuse to sell it. As for the hospital bill, that was worth an extra sigh of relief.

"Thank you," she whispered. "That makes me feel a lot better."

"No problem," he said, his slow smile easing the tension. "Takis asked how you were, and I said Athina might like to drop by for her lesson after school. Socrates will come here straight after work, if that's alright. The contest begins next week, and he's getting nervous."

Summer nodded. At least it would occupy her scattered thoughts, give her something to do and ease some of the guilt that so many people were doing so much for her.

～

On Friday morning, Summer sat by her hospital bed, crutches by her side, drumming her fingers on the cold metal arm of the chair as she waited for the doctor to discharge her.

In the last three days, she'd spent every spare minute either giving English lessons or hobbling around this wretched room. While it was good to make some significant progress with Athina and Socrates, she was itching to get back. In two weeks, she had to finish the house, put it on the market and get it sold.

Costa saw her every day, and she'd tried to be grateful but keep her distance. She'd resolved not to mention the magazine pictures—what did it really matter anyway? She'd avoid him as much as possible in the next two weeks, sidestep his concern, and ignore the physical pull his body seemed to exert over hers.

The renovations would soon be complete, and a quick sale could be imminent. The estate agent had dropped into the hospital the night before, and it was a relief that she'd signed the contract to put the house on the market. Soon there would be no need to stay married and she could apply for a dissolution. There was no reason to put it off any longer; her time on the island was ending.

When the doctor had finished checking her over, he handed her a bottle of painkillers and her discharge papers and said he'd let her know when the taxi would be there to collect her.

"Taxi?" Hurt caught her off guard. Costa hadn't come to pick her up? He hadn't mentioned it yesterday...she'd just assumed...

She thanked the doctor, but said she'd wait for the taxi in the lobby. The more exercise she could get the better.

Her spirits lifted during the thirty-minute drive back to the village. The taxi driver recognized her from the wedding feast and chatted about the wonderful ceremony and how he hoped he could marry off all his daughters in the same style.

They stopped as a goatherd led his snowy charges across the road, and when they were past, Summer rolled down her window to breathe in the beautiful outside scents. With a pang, she realized she'd missed her little house, the scent of the orange grove, even the rustling in the roof.

The driver pulled up as close to her lane as he could. She was surprised to see her front door open and even more astonished to see two small green bushes in bright blue containers on either side of the door. Had Costa put them there?

The taxi driver wanted to help her inside, but she was determined to do this herself and slung her small backpack over her shoulder. Costa would see how capable she was, and that she was ready to finish the job she'd come here to complete.

As the taxi moved away, she made her way up the cobbled lane and through the front door, pushing it behind her until it clicked. She froze, her hand to her heart. Was this her house?

The walls were a brilliant white, all plastered and newly painted. Everything shone in their reflected glow.

To the back of the room, a brand new kitchen stood with gleaming benches, a table and four matching chairs, and even a stove in the corner. It looked complete, welcoming.

Like a home.

Slowly, she moved into the room. Warmth began in her stomach and trailed up her body. Then she noticed the floor. Not only was it now wooden, but thick rugs lay everywhere, and she wanted to dig her toes into the wool. The house was everything she'd dreamed it could be. The thought of Costa listening to how she imagined her home might be brought the sting of tears to her eyes.

Then she remembered. *Money.*

Of course, this was easy for him to do. He was a millionaire—maybe a billionaire. Why wouldn't he just go out and get someone to install a new kitchen, have someone deliver a few rugs? The shine immediately dulled.

She thought of him doing the laboring downstairs, shirt off, muscles tense and rippling, and she forced her mind to reject those images as her lungs constricted. But the plastering, organizing the tradespeople. Why would he do all of that if he was, as the nurse had said, one of the richest men in Greece?

Why hadn't he simply paid for everything?

His silhouette moved past the window, and she had just a moment to compose herself.

"Hi," he said as he came through the door, wiping his hands on his rolled-up chinos. The glow on his face hinted that he'd been hard at work, and for a moment, Summer felt the pull of him again—that he was there, in her house, still helping her was too much to think about. "I'm sorry I wasn't at the hospital to collect you," he said. "I had to wait for a contractor to sign off."

"You've been very busy," she wheezed, and reached for her inhaler.

"Not just me—"

"I really appreciate it, Costa." She took a puff of medicine and leaned heavily on one of her crutches, gazing around in wonder. "I don't know how I'm ever going to repay you."

Costa moved forward with a chair and placed it carefully behind her. "The place is far from finished," he said, his voice full of pride. "The downstairs is almost complete, though." He walked into the kitchen. "The roof still needs to be done, and the whitewashing of the outside will take some time. Coffee?"

She nodded, then sat down heavily, more than just her

ankle aching. She could either go on like this, pretending she wasn't confused, that she wasn't smothering under a blanket of questions and concerns, or she could be blunt.

"Who are you, Costa?"

He ran water into the pot from a shiny new faucet, then looked at her, a gentle smile teasing his mouth. He whistled out a breath before answering. "That's a very direct question. What do you mean?"

She stretched out her good leg, wishing she could scratch the permanent itch beneath the plaster on the other.

"I've been honest with you about why I'm here, what drives me, and I've opened up to you about my life. I don't feel you've done any of that with me and I'd like to know why." As soon as her words were out, she realized how ungrateful she sounded, but she couldn't take them back.

He put the coffeepot on the flame and his expression didn't change; he gave nothing away as he watched her.

"I've told you who I am. I'm just a Greek boy from an island village who works overseas and who's back for the summer. I've told you about my relationship with my father, and why I needed to leave here. I've been as honest with you as I'm able."

She rubbed her temple. "But you're not just anyone, are you?" He was concentrating on the coffee, so she continued. "Why, for example, does everyone call you Kirieh...Mr. Nicoliedies?"

He pulled the pot off, waited a moment before putting it back on the flame.

"Those people, mostly the old men from the village, see me as different to them," he said quietly. She knew he was telling the truth, trying to be honest. "I told you they have a certain criterion for success and when they believe someone has achieved it they put them on a pedestal."

"And that success would be...having the lifestyle? The money?"

"Yes." He poured coffee into the cups and brought one to her, then sat on the floor a few feet away. "Having a lot of money."

"So why didn't you tell me?" This was easier than she'd thought. He wasn't trying to hide anything, except why he'd needed a translation job. "To ensure I wouldn't try to stay married to you? I wouldn't make a claim?"

His dark, fathomless eyes held hers. "I didn't think it was important to tell you I had money."

"Not just the money—the lifestyle, the status. Don't you think that's something someone you become friends with...?" She stopped, wary of giving away the hurt and confusion inside her.

She took a sip of coffee, aware his gaze remained fixed on her. She may as well say everything. "In that magazine, the glossy one I was looking at in the hospital..."

"Was a picture of me?"

"Yes."

"Was it a good one?"

She lifted her gaze to his—his eyes danced. She ignored the question, determined to be hurt that he hadn't been more honest with her but struggling to stay wary when he looked at her with sparkling eyes. "It surprised me. You hadn't given me the impression that's what you are about."

He put his cup on the floor and leaned forward, his forearms resting on his knees, hands clasped. "Summer, that's because it's not what I'm about."

She leaned back, uncomfortable with the closeness her body craved. His ring of confidence she'd noticed that first day was threatening to turn her accusations into whispers. War was erupting inside her. One second she wanted to fall into his arms—hug him, kiss him, tell him she'd never felt

155

about anyone the way she felt about him. And the next she wanted to hammer board after board across her fragile heart so she wouldn't be devastated when their time here was over.

"It's part of my life, sure, but not something that defines me. Having money means people always want a piece of you, to be seen with you, to socialize and do business with you, but it holds no more meaning in my life than any other requirement of my business. That fact that you haven't known those things about me has made my time with you...priceless."

She tried to ignore the intimate direction of the conversation. "So all those parties and red carpets," *and the women*, "are a chore?" The hand holding her coffee cup trembled.

He chuckled. "Not always, no, but they don't add any meaning to my life either." He rubbed a hand across his jaw. "Summer, your mother taught me to dream big, to believe anything was possible, but she also taught me we are responsible for our actions, for the way we treat others and the way we treat the world. I've always followed her principle that it's a person's integrity that makes them rich, not dollars in the bank."

As soon as he'd said the words, Costa knew what a hypocrite he was and inwardly cringed. Not only had their marriage lacked integrity in the beginning, but he still hadn't told her the whole truth. He'd been determined to tell her everything, knowing that in doing so he'd be able to help her heal the negative impression she had about her mother, but the time had never been right.

He had to find a way to tell Summer the truth without betraying his promise to Caroline. She sat stiffly in the chair, and he fought the impulse to pull her close and whisper how much she meant to him. But he couldn't, not with such a heavy weight between them.

"I don't get it," she blurted. "How you can put so much store into the words of my mother when her actions clearly upset people in this village? How does sending me back here to pick up all the pieces of her life...how does that show integrity?"

"We're all flawed, Summer. Just because she was your mother doesn't mean she was immune to making mistakes."

She scoffed. "From what I've seen from the reactions of people in this village, they were pretty big mistakes, Costa."

He inched forward. He burned to touch her, to have the closeness they'd had only days ago when she'd lain in his arms—when she hadn't known who he was other than a man she wanted. "I know you believe the decisions she made when she was sick were mistaken, but don't you think you could celebrate the fact that she *had* such strong convictions? There are so many people in this world who are too frightened to *have* a belief, let alone follow it."

Instantly her eyes flared. "I did celebrate some of my mother's convictions, but I can't condone the negative impact she's clearly had on some of the families here."

He leaned closer, desperate to make her understand. "That's not the way it was at all. Okay, my father might have believed it, but the majority of the people in the village thought your mother was incredible. They *loved* her."

She stilled. "Are you sure, because..."

"Yes." Her body was tight, anxiety coming off her in waves. Wait. What did she mean because? "Has somebody said something to you?"

"At the wedding..." She looked down at her small hands clasped tightly in her lap, knuckles white. "A woman spoke to me."

Costa's heart hammered.

Her gaze flicked back to his, and his heart bottomed out when he saw her glassy eyes. "She was crying, Costa, sobbing because her nephew and others had gone away, all because of my mother. You should've seen the way she looked at me."

"Are you sure she said that?" It confused him. People in the village had loved Caroline, especially after what had happened.

"Did she speak English, this woman?"

Now she was wringing her hands. "No, not very well. She just said her nephew, Michali, and some other people had gone, gone, gone and it was very bad."

"Is that all she said?"

"She was too upset to say anything else." She leaned a little closer. "So, can you see why I don't buy any of this stuff about convictions? It's all very well to live the way you want, but when it destroys the lives of others...it's plain wrong."

It was time to tell her, time to come clean. It was true he owed Caroline everything, true that she'd asked him to keep secrets, but he was sure she wouldn't want to see her daughter in such pain.

"Summer, maybe that woman—"

"No, Costa." She flicked the air as if to wipe his words away with her hand. "I'll not have you try to sanitize everything for me again. It's time you and I faced up to facts. Apart from meeting you, everything on this island has been one sorry mess after another, and I can see it clearly now. If it wasn't for you, if I hadn't been lucky enough to have you to help me..." Her words slowed until she spoke one painstaking breath at a time. "If...I...hadn't...met..."

Her eyes widened and a shadow of bewilderment enveloped her features. He wanted to stop it, but realized there was no going back, that he should have told her before she...

"But luck had nothing to do with it. Did it, Costa?"

Suddenly her cup slid, closely followed by the saucer, and they both smashed on the newly laid floor. Unflinching, Summer spoke even more precisely. "She asked you to come, didn't she?"

He moved closer, reached for her icy hand, but she wrenched it away. Pain transformed her beautiful face, and he wanted to whisper the words away, turn it all around. She was dissolving before his eyes, and he wanted nothing more than to pull her to him and take away her pain.

"Costa? She asked you to come, didn't she?" Hurt scored every word as she continued, the words tumbling out of her mouth. "Of course, that's it...Why else would you want to help someone like me? *Marry* someone like me? Was it some way for you to pay her back for all the crazy ideas she put in your head?

She spat the words like poison, and he felt each as an individual blow.

"What sort of integrity do *you* have if you present yourself as one thing when really you're another?" She struggled to get up, a curtain of horror transforming her face, but her crutch clattered onto the shiny wooden floor.

"Summer?" He reached out, touched the delicate skin on her arm and felt the goose bumps before she dragged her arm away, flinching at his touch.

"Why didn't you *tell* me? How could you go on letting me think this was all a convenient coincidence? That you wanted to help me because you...liked me, not because I was some agreed-upon obligation?"

Her words wobbled, and she gasped for breath between them. "Was getting me into bed part of the favor, too?"

He struggled to breathe as her words slammed into him.

"Did my mother ask you to bed me so I wouldn't be the frigid, driven daughter she was ashamed of?"

"No, Summer. God, no." Once more he caught her

elbows, tried to stop her self-destruction, but she wrenched herself away from him.

Now there were tears, and Summer swiped at them savagely with the insides of her wrists. She was distraught, lost, abandoned.

And it was all his fault.

CHAPTER ELEVEN

Trying to swallow back her treacherous tears, Summer scraped her chair across the wooden floor, desperate to get away from him.

How could she have believed the words he'd whispered when she'd lain in his arms, their bodies entwined as if they belonged together? Every cell in her body cringed—in shame because of what she'd wished for with Costa, and in anger at what he and her mother had done.

"Why? That's all I want to know." She locked her jaw so her bottom lip wouldn't tremble, her body weak after the adrenaline rush of her realization.

He stayed where he was, balanced on the edge of his chair but holding her gaze. "You have every right to be angry, Summer."

"You're not wrong there." She held her chin higher, hoping it would ease the ache in her jaw as she desperately tried to stop the tears.

"Your mother asked me to come here and make sure everything worked out for you."

"Because I was incapable of organizing my sad and sorry life?"

"No."

She exhaled sharply. "Then, why?"

He rubbed his hands across his cheeks, then stood and walked to a window. The sun shone from behind him so she couldn't see his features. Shoulders hunched, he stuffed his hands deep into his pockets. For a second he looked almost vulnerable.

"She didn't want you dealing with everything here on your own."

Again she let out a sharp breath. "But that's what she didn't understand about me. Since I moved to Brentwood Bay at eighteen, I've built a community around me. Neighbors who check in on me. Girlfriends who came round as soon as Mom passed. Workmates who've texted me every day I've been here."

"But coming to a foreign country after your mother had died, being presented with renovating and selling the house." He spread his arms wide in emphasis. "She knew what a huge undertaking it would be."

"So she asked you to come here and marry me?" The words came out in a wheezy rasp of disbelief.

"Of course not." Softness flickered in his eyes, "I hadn't thought about the foreign renovation financial rule, as I'm sure she didn't. I'd made a promise to her, and I had to see it through. The marriage had to happen."

"Then why the secrets?" She rubbed her temples. "Why couldn't you just turn up and say, 'Your mother's sent me to look after you.'"

He turned his face slightly to the side, and she saw the smallest grin. "Perhaps because she knew you'd send me back to where I came from."

"Because I can't ask for help?"

"Partly." He shrugged. "But also because she wanted you to do this project yourself. She wanted you to have a sense of achievement. I think she also hoped you'd see the beauty of a slower lifestyle."

It all sounded very practical and sickeningly patronizing. "And what did she want *you* to learn from this exercise?"

A frown played on his forehead as he crossed his arms. "What do you mean?"

"You don't think she didn't have a hidden agenda for you *too*, do you?"

He started. "No. She knew I'd do anything for her, so she asked me for a favor."

"A favor that involved you spending time away from the glitz and glamor of a life with money so you could reconnect with your roots?"

He was quiet for a moment, his fingers kneading his bicep.

She pushed on. "Don't you think *your* salvation was part of the plan as well? Getting your hands dirty, playing the good Samaritan—she had us both pegged for a lifestyle revolution."

"Maybe there's something more, Summer. I'm going to ask my father about something that might change—"

She slammed her palms up in a furious stop sign. "No, Costa." Suddenly she felt more in control than she had for a long time. "Enough. That's all I can process for one day. Please do me the courtesy of keeping any more little gems about my mother to yourself."

His mouth opened as if to speak, then he nodded, a muscle pulsing at his jaw.

"There's absolutely nothing more I want to hear about Mom, nothing you could say that would alter the betrayal I feel right now from both of you."

He sank to a crouch, his back against the wall he'd plastered. "Okay, but when you're ready to talk more, I'll be here. Summer, there's got to be something I can do—something to make up for the way this has all turned out so badly."

"But why is it bad?" She rubbed her throbbing temple. "Hasn't it all gone completely to plan? You've carried out your part of the bargain; I've been completely in the dark. It's all happened the way Mom wanted. I'd say that was a success, wouldn't you?"

His eyes narrowed, and she could see he was hurt by the malice in her voice. "It all seemed reasonable until I..." He rubbed his hands across his face but stayed silent.

Summer sent a death glare at her foot in the cast. It throbbed in reply. "I think you realize she's manipulated both of us, tried to carry on her beliefs by forcing us to confront our own. You've got to hand it to her, I suppose. She was really clever to pull this all off."

Her breathing steadied as she recognized he was very much in the same position as she was. Her mother had planned this so they'd both be forced to take a long, hard look at their lifestyles. "So what do we do now?"

Costa pushed his legs out in front of him as he sat on the floor, his face strained. "We finish this place."

"Do you think we can?" She'd been desperately hoping he'd say that; there was absolutely no way she could finish this on her own, and they'd worked so well together. Achieved so much.

His eyes softened. "Of course we can, Summer. I'm sorry you feel betrayed by your mom and me, but please know I'll fix this."

For the first time in a long time, Costa felt out of control. He wanted to pull Summer to him, tell her she did things to his body and mind—confusing things, impossible things, wonderful things.

When he'd sat by her hospital bed and waited for her to wake, something had changed in him. Suddenly the "big picture" he'd clung to had become microscopic. It was no longer about empire building and corporate castles, always looking for the next deal. Now it was just about him and a hurting, haunting woman he wanted to spend the rest of his life with.

Another thought played in his head. Was Summer right? Had Caroline planned this whole thing as a life-changing event for both of them? If she had, he hadn't seen it coming —but suddenly it all made sense.

She'd made him see that he'd neglected his roots by making him return to them and see their beauty and strength.

"What do I have to do" he asked, "to make it up to you? To make you see I never meant to hurt you?"

She chewed her lip without looking at him and shrugged one delicate shoulder. "I don't know, Costa. I can understand why you did it; you thought you were paying back a debt to Mom. I just wish I didn't feel as if I'd been used in some social experiment."

He tested a grin. "It hasn't been all bad, has it?"

She lifted her eyes to his, and this time her gaze was soft. "No, of course it hasn't been all bad."

"You've learned new things, made new friends, and you're on track to sell the house and live out your dream." His chest hollowed as he imagined her thousands of miles away.

"Yes, but in the process I feel as if I've lost a...friend." She looked down as her voice wobbled.

Without thinking, he was up off the floor and kneeling in front of her. Carefully, he reached for her hand. "Look at me Summer."

Slowly her eyelids lifted, and he was trapped in an ocean of blue.

"I never imagined that coming back home and getting involved...with this project, with you, would have such an effect on me." Her eyes became glossy, but he continued. "When we made love, I felt as if I had come home to something. To *someone*."

Her throat moved in a swallow.

"I can't believe you don't feel something too." He squeezed her hand, hoping for a moment of togetherness.

"I can't," she whispered. His heart dropped, but he waited. "You're a traveler—in a funny way, just as much of a drifter as my mom. I want more than a summer romance with a man on the other side of the world."

She withdrew her hands and turned away. Shutting him out of her heart.

～

Later that afternoon, Summer sat on one of the large stones at the side of the house and watched as Costa mended the dreaded ladder rung. The day was warm and a single drop of sweat trickled from his hairline and down his cheek. The light scent of oranges on a dying breeze tickled her nose.

His confession that she meant something to him had taken her aback, and for a moment she'd believed it with all her heart until finally reason took over. They were two different people on two different paths.

It was best they try to get back on some professional footing. It sucked that she could no longer help with the renovation, but at least she could be outside. And watching Costa was very easy. She tracked another bead of sweat.

"How can you afford so much time off work with your busy lifestyle?" She tugged at her sunhat. He'd almost finished with the ladder and had promised to check on the swallows.

"I have good people running my businesses for me," he said. "They don't need me around much and if it's urgent they'll email, text or phone, and since I don't take a lot of holidays, this is quite special."

Quite special.

"In what way?"

"I've enjoyed being back, much more than I thought I would." His broad shoulders pulled the fabric of his T-shirt as he worked, and she had to drag her gaze back to his face. "During the evenings you were in the hospital, I spent time with my father and things feel...different."

Summer spread her skirt out across the rock so she could feel more warmth on her good leg.

"In what way?"

"We've been talking." He placed the ladder against the side of the house. "I'm going up now. If I haven't fixed this rung properly, you'll need to carry me up to the hospital." A playful smile teased his full lips. Lips she remembered kissing a line along her breastbone, up her neck, playing soft across her cheek.

She fought the images in her mind. "Is that what you did?"

His foot on the rung, he stilled and turned to her clearly puzzled. "What?"

"Carried me all the way to the hospital?"

He started up the ladder without answering. "I built a box for the birds that fits in the ceiling space and put the nest back there," he said without looking at her. "It means you won't hear them moving around and I won't have to mend the hole in the roof where they've been entering."

"Do you think I'm crazy?" she said, suddenly realizing what he must think about her obsession with the birds.

Everyone, even swallows, deserved a home; a place to come back to where they felt safe and loved.

"Only a little."

The slightest grin danced at the corner of his mouth, and a thread of relief unfurled inside her.

"What can you see? And be careful when you lean over." Her heart beat a little faster. "I'm not sure how long it would take me to carry you to the hospital."

A swallow flew out from under the eaves.

"They're back!" Summer cried, feeling ridiculously over-joyed. "Is the nest okay?"

Costa leaned across the roof, removed a tile and was quiet for a moment before replacing the tile and climbing down the ladder.

"What did you see?" she asked, her heart thumping. "Is the nest still there?"

He turned to her. The small smile she'd seen a few moments ago was now fully fledged and it sailed straight into her heart.

"The nest's still there." He took a step toward her. "But I'll need to fix the tiles over the top of it."

"That would be great. Maybe we could get Socrates to check out all the roof tiles, and maybe you could check the spouting."

A small line settled on his brow, and he cleared his throat. "I've been thinking." Looking down, he scuffed his boot through the dust. "Socrates and Takis can finish their jobs—white-washing the outside and fixing the last of the walls. I could leave things to them if that makes you feel more comfortable."

Summer swallowed. No. That wasn't what she wanted. Not at all.

"Why would you leave now, before we've put it on the market, before we get a sale? Costa, as Mom clearly knew, I could have done none of this without you. If you can spare a final week, I really want us to see this through to the end. Together."

He looked up again, his eyes brighter. "I suppose you're right. It's certainly been a challenge for me these last few weeks."

Summer thought about the bed, the new kitchen and the shiny new floor he'd put down, all the windows he'd fixed, and dread swirled through her. "Can you last another week or two? I'm pretty hopeless at everything." She stared down at the cast on her foot. "I'm not sure I could communicate very well with Socrates and Takis."

She looked back at him and he gave her the slow, sexy smile that made her pulse quicken and her wish there was a future for them.

"If you can stand having me around, then I'd love to help you finish."

Summer sat on a flat rock, one slim brown leg and one fat plaster cast poking out from under a white skirt that skimmed her hips and dropped to just below her knees. A blue shirt accentuated her amazing eyes and showed a hint of creamy cleavage he should not be noticing. Why hadn't he told her everything he knew about Caroline right from the moment the secret became too much to keep from her?

At first, he'd put it down to his pledge to Caroline, but now he realized it had been about wanting to shelter Summer, protect her from any more hurt.

The memory of her sated and lying in his arms played in his mind. The way she'd whispered his name, how she'd clung to him, their legs entwined, her hair fanned on his chest. And the remembered terror of finding her crumpled on the ground stabbed him in the heart.

She'd grown since her arrival. His first impression had been that she was wary, unworldly, but she'd grown in strength and confidence. He loved the way she'd now wave to Petro as he passed by each morning and call out to him in her wonky Greek. She joked with Takis in sign language and sang lyrics to Socrates in English, high-fiving him when he got the words right. She smiled more, laughed more, and he wanted to drink in all she had to give.

She fiddled with her hem. "So, do you think you'll continue talking things through with your father?"

"Yes." He thought of a conversation he'd had with his dad the night before. For the very first time, the old man had asked him about his job, his property developments, and he'd seemed interested in what Costa did. "My father seems different since his conversation with you at the church."

Summer smiled and turned a little on the rock. "That's great."

"Perhaps he's realized his children were always going to be people who needed to stretch their wings. I think it surprised him to learn you weren't trying to change things with the house, and that you respected the laws of the village. He got a different impression of you that day."

"That was only because you talked me into it." Summer grinned. "Remember when I first arrived and asked you to help me bend the rules? You were very adamant that I couldn't."

"Maybe I've learned something too. I left when I was young. Couldn't wait to get away. Maybe I lost sight of my heritage and my place on the island."

They were silent for a moment as the tension between them eased. "How will you manage in the house?" he asked, nodding at her leg. "Showering, cooking, all those sorts of things."

The faintest blush touched Summer's cheeks, and for just a moment she seemed lost for words. "I guess I will need help after all."

～

For the rest of the afternoon, Summer sat in the cool of the kitchen while Socrates, Takis and Costa worked on the roof. The door was open and a warm breeze laced with a sweet, peppery fragrance wafted in.

When she'd come back inside, she'd found a small dish filled with the pink beads that Costa had found throughout the house, and now she sat threading them onto a piece of fishing line. The unexpected kindness of his gift brought a lump to her throat. He knew what having these meant to her.

As she threaded each bead on the fishing line, she marveled at how things had changed since she'd found that very first one. This wasn't frightening any more. No longer was she overwhelmed by the state of the house or the monumental task of the renovation. With Costa's help, she'd complete the crazy task her mother had set, and then she'd never need to come here again. No more boxes in the ceiling, no more need to be married...

"*Yah-sas.*" Someone called out as they passed the door on their way down the lane and she waved out to them. Given what she'd learned from Costa's father and the woman at the wedding, why were people still friendly toward her?

Another plate of food from Yianni sat on the counter, ready for their dinner, and more oranges were piled high in the beautiful turquoise bowl. The feeling of friendship and neighborhood warmed her, and she battled with a sadness that she'd never return here. Once she had the agreement on

'Safe Anchorage' finalised, she'd need to work overtime to afford the mortgage payments. There would be nothing left for overseas travel.

Athina came for her lesson and left, ecstatic that she'd mastered some complex grammar rules and was now ready for her exams. Socrates, too, had learned his lyrics and wouldn't need any more help from her.

She finished the beads and was contemplating whether it was time for dinner when Socrates and Takis waved their goodbyes and Costa materialized.

"I'm going." He shrugged into a denim jacket. "I'm spending some time with Dad. I'll come back later."

A dove's call carried on the early evening breeze and Summer suddenly realized how late it was. "I'm sorry you had to work so long."

He stuffed his hands into his pockets, a satisfied smile tipping his lips. "We made a lot of progress. Two more days and the roof will be complete."

She moved to get up, but he waved her back down. "You should rest."

"But surely there's something I can do to help. I feel like a cast sheep, sitting here all day."

He stared at her hard, then his face cleared. "You could start whitewashing the outside. If you sat on a chair and did what you could reach—that would help a lot."

"I can't wait." Her brain scrambled, trying to think of something else to say. She didn't want him to leave. "Athina's mother sent over a bottle of wine. Would you like a glass?"

He hesitated. "You should really get some rest."

"One glass? So we can talk. I'd love your company."

He gave a hesitant grin but walked into the kitchen. "Will you be able to fly like that?" he asked, flicking a glance at her encased leg as he took two glasses and poured the wine.

"Yes," Summer said. "The doctor said he can give me a

temporary cast for the flight home and I'll have my foot checked when I get back." Back to the town she knew like the back of her hand, the "safe anchorage" that would realize her dream. "Thank you so much for paying for those specialists to come from Athens. I don't know —." She tried to keep the tremor out of her voice, but failed.

"I didn't pay them."

"Oh..." Did that mean she'd have to pay for them? "Well, all this then," she said, smoothing the soft cotton cover of the chair she sat on. "Thanks for buying—"

"I didn't pay for any of this either."

She stared at him "Wait. I don't understand."

He sat the wineglass in front of her, his fingers brushing hers and the usual sparkle shot up her arm.

"The people from the village."

She gazed around the room, trying to piece the meaning of his words together. "But the bed, the linen..?"

He stuffed his hands deep in his pockets. "Neighbors, shopkeepers from the village."

None of this made sense. She'd guessed from the very beginning that Costa had money, and now she knew he had mountains of it. Why would he let other people do all this? "I don't understand."

"Why I didn't just order it all?" He sat on the chair opposite.

Summer bit her lip and her cheeks burned. Hearing him say it made her assumptions seem crass. Why *should* he pay for things for her?

"Your mother asked me not to." He took a mouthful of wine and his brow creased. "At first I thought it was because she wanted you to survive on your own so you'd have a real sense of achievement."

"Sounds like Mom."

His dark eyes held her. "But now I don't think that's what it was about at all."

She shifted back in the chair. "What do you mean?"

"I've been thinking about what you said, about your mom having an agenda for me. I don't know why, but it hadn't occurred to me at all. I guess she knew I had money, but we never really spoke about it. I certainly didn't see that she had a plan for me. But now I think you were right."

She nodded encouragement for him to go on, her heart skipping in her chest.

"Having to get things done without money has been quite a challenge for me in the last couple of weeks. Everything I did to help you had to be from my actions, not my cash, that's what your mother stipulated. It was hard in the beginning. For example, when I wanted to get you a bed, I had to go and talk to people, re-establish relationships I hadn't visited for a long time. And not just reconnecting, but forging new relationships too. Even the simple act of going into the orchard to pick oranges for you was something I hadn't done for years."

"And did you enjoy it?"

His genuine smile melted a part of her heart she hadn't realized was frozen. Her mom's cancer diagnosis, the long shifts in the hospital saving money for her treatment, the soaring hope they could have a mother/daughter relationship all dashed when her mother had wanted to do things differently—everything had contributed to a numbness that was starting to leave her.

"Yes, I did. It's easy to lose sight of the importance of relationships when you're in business and the majority of the people you deal with work for you." He paused. "I guess being here has been a bit of a wake-up call."

Now it was her turn to pause. "Do you think Mom knew that about you?"

"She never asked much about my life when we texted or emailed." He shrugged. "Maybe she had a sense that although I'd achieved a lot, I wasn't always happy."

Was he happy now? She hoped so with all her heart.

"But what about all of this? Surely you paid for something?"

He shook his head. "None of it. When the villagers heard what had happened to you, they rallied around like I couldn't believe with labor or materials. It was all donated."

"That's amazing," Summer breathed.

"And when some of the men heard that a photojournalist had arrived on the ferry looking for a tabloid scandal or a compromising photo of me, they went to the wharf and firmly persuaded him that chasing me and a story wasn't a good idea."

"I'm sorry," she said, startling herself with the outburst.

His eyes hooked her and reeled her in. "What for?"

The answer came from somewhere deep within. "For doubting you. For not understanding why it was so important for you to keep the secret my mother asked you to." She took a sip of wine.

"You felt betrayed. You were hurt." His voice was undoing her. "It was understandable."

From within the dormant fire of her heart, something suddenly flickered. She looked up and the creases of concern she'd seen in his face moments ago softened. "So you're not sorry you came back?" She spoke quietly, her hands tightening around the stem of the wineglass.

"Of course not. Although I came back because your mom asked me to, I've discovered a lot while I've been here."

She didn't know how to ask him what that was, and as if sensing her internal debate, he continued talking. "I can see what my father loves so much about this place." He looked out the window, across the orange grove. "I used to think it

175

was a sign of weakness, my parents wanting to stay here, build their lives here. Now I see something different."

Summer almost didn't speak for fear of breaking the spell. Her voice was a whisper. "What?"

"It's all about relationships, and community, and working together. That doesn't always happen in business—in fact, often the more prosperous the business, the more the community is eroded as people work longer and longer hours with more and more demands."

"So you could see yourself back here, as mayor of the village, just as tradition dictates?"

Costa turned to her, his eyes deeper and darker than she'd ever seen them before. "Only if I had the right person by my side."

CHAPTER TWELVE

*S*ummer managed to limp all the way to the *kafenion* the next morning. Not only did she want some exercise after sitting around for so long, but she wanted to thank Yianni for the food he'd sent her in the last few weeks. The limitless generosity of the villagers touched her heart.

As soon as she arrived in the square, the old men rallied around. One pulled up a table so she wouldn't need to walk so far, another brought one chair for her to sit on and another for her foot.

"*Kalimera, Yianni*," she called as she saw the shop owner rushing toward her. And when he'd shaken her hand in both of his and offered a string of platitudes, she said, "*Café ke rizogalo, sas parakalo*," surprising herself with how readily the words rolled off her tongue. He beamed and gave the slightest bow before rushing off. Her mouth watered in anticipation of his rich coffee and exquisite rice pudding.

From various tables, men called greetings and Summer smiled and nodded back. After everything she'd learned in the last few days, her acceptance by the villagers brought a lump to her throat.

She thought back to Costa's words the night before.

Did he really feel something for her? One part of her desperately wanted to believe him, wanted the closeness of the relationship they'd shared before. Another part kept remembering her mom's photo and what it represented—transience, emptiness. She sighed and shook her head. She owed it to herself to follow her dream, her vision of a stable and permanent life for herself and, hopefully one day, her children.

The memory of the passionate night with Costa crept into her mind. The dream of a life with him touched her for a moment; another time, another place, what if...?

"Good morning." She was jolted from her daydream by Costa's father, who stood beside her. She tried to scramble up, but the firm, warm hand on her shoulder gently guided her back down to her seat.

"I do not wish to disturb you," he said in his rich accent, "but if you have a moment there is something I would like to say to you."

Summer nodded and managed a smile as her heart beat faster. Was he going to berate her? Tell her more about her mother? She shifted uncomfortably in her seat.

Yianni brought the coffee and rice pudding and, after a quick exchange with Costa's father, left them alone.

Summer's finger hovered over the cup handle.

"Please go ahead and drink," he said. "This will not take long."

Trying to hold her hand steady, Summer took a sip of coffee.

"I must apologize for the way I spoke to you at the wedding," he began. "They were the words of a confused old man who should learn to stay closer to home when he is looking for someone to blame for his troubles." He held one palm to his chest as if to emphasize his sincerity.

"It's okay—"

"It is not okay, it is inexcusable. I was speaking about a past that doesn't exist now and maybe never did, feelings that are so old they've forgotten their purpose."

Thoughts bubbled and churned, but nothing meaningful reached her lips, so she just nodded.

"I should have thanked you instead."

Summer blinked and put the coffee cup down.

"Thanked me?"

The old man placed his black and gold worry beads on the table and they glinted in the sun. "For bringing my son home. For giving him time in his old village. For him visiting me after so many years." His hand swiped the air. "Oh, I'm not foolish enough to think I was the reason for his return, but I can certainly see a change in him since he's been here."

Summer stroked the side of the cup. "You know, it wasn't me. It was my mom who asked Costa to come here."

He pushed one bead on its chain, then another. "I know," he said quietly. "She was a remarkable woman, your mother, with views ahead of our time. It's only taken me thirty years to realize it. I even learned to speak English when I could see the benefits for the village." His smile was self-deprecating. "And it seems to me that her daughter is made of the same very strong material."

"I don't know about that," Summer said. "Perhaps if I'd tried to understand my mother better, I wouldn't be so lost now she's gone." The emotional power of the words she'd just uttered hit her like a punch to the gut, and the old man must have sensed it as he reached out and touched her hand.

"You have helped bring great joy to our family," he said smiling. "My son has changed in the last few weeks and I know he has developed powerful feelings for you."

Summer inadvertently swallowed a hot mouthful of

coffee and tried to divert the shock at his words by asking a question. "In what way has he changed?"

"He has a new appreciation of the village. The way he's interacted with everyone to get things done on the house, I think it's given him a whole new lease on life."

"But only because he was bound by my mother. She wanted him to help me sell the house."

"I know. He has told me everything and I think, perhaps, your mother was a very clever woman."

Summer smiled. "I like to think so, although sometimes it wasn't easy to see."

"I must admit, I was very suspicious when she came here with her different ideas. It certainly challenged the way some of us saw the world. Of course, we always wanted what was best for our children, but it was difficult to hear them say they didn't want to remain on the island."

Summer was warming to this proud old man. He was obviously a thinker, someone who was deeply touched by those around him. It must have taken a great deal of courage for him to be opening up to her.

She took a sip of coffee and watched a group of kids playing under the trees. "But you couldn't support what she was doing at the time."

"Maybe not, but I can see that perhaps she had a plan for my son, and perhaps for you, too. Something that was greater than any of us could imagine."

They sat in silence for a few minutes, Summer letting the touch of the sun heat her back and the warmth of Costa's father's words touch her heart.

"She was loved, your mother," he said quietly. "By the entire village, and they accepted her as one of theirs."

"Then why did she leave?" Summer asked. "I assumed it was because she'd alienated people with her views."

A shadow passed over the older man's face, and for the

first time he avoided her gaze and instead stared out across the bay. "Something happened just before your mother left, something I am not in a position to discuss with you, but it touched the people here deeply."

Questions began to form rapidly in her mind, one on top of the other like a building storm.

The coffee cup rattled against the table when she put it down. "What sort of something? What do you mean?"

He picked up the worry beads and held them tight, his eyes softening with emotion. "You must ask Costa. He asked the same question last night and I told him the story. I'd prefer him to explain it to you, my dear."

The effort to get down the hill on crutches was almost more difficult than going up, but Summer was desperate to get back to the house and Costa. His father had offered to deliver her there himself, but she wanted to talk to Costa without an audience. One more day to finish whitewashing and the house would be finished. One more day and Costa would be gone. And that thought pierced her heart.

If there was something else about her mother, why hadn't he told her? It was true she'd told him she didn't want to hear any more but... Nothing he could say now could be more of a shock than what he'd already said.

He was painting the back of the house. She could hear the murmur of Socrates and Takis talking from the other side.

He stood as soon as he saw her, his face more tanned than she'd seen it before, more relaxed. She noticed tiny smile lines etched into the skin by his eyes and she took a quick breath.

"You weren't here when I got up this morning." He grinned. "I was beginning to get worried." Slowly, the smile that took up most of his face faded. "Summer, what is it? What's wrong?"

"I've just had a coffee with your father."

A frown formed across his forehead. "What has he said? Has he upset you? I thought he was beginning to understand things. We spoke about—"

"He didn't upset me. He said some lovely things about me, about my mother, and about you."

"What things?" He took her by the arm and she felt the familiar struggle, wanting him and not wanting him. For a moment, she leaned into him as he guided her to a rock and helped her sit. His warm, muscled arm touched the skin of her arm and she shivered. He laid her crutches on the ground and sat on the opposite rock.

"He thanked me, for bringing you here."

He swallowed, his Adam's apple bobbing.

"He said that?" He rubbed his jaw, stubble rasping as surprise flittered across his face.

"He said he's seen a change in you since you've been back." He didn't speak but stared at her, so she carried on. "He didn't hate my mother, Costa. He said that he thinks she planned for you to have this challenge."

"What made him think that?" His brow furrowed in question as the breeze ruffled his hair.

"He said he's watched you mixing with the locals, having to rely on the help of others to get things done, and he thinks you've learned a lot."

The smallest lift in his lips told her he liked what she was saying. "Really?"

"Yes, but he said something else, something that didn't make any sense to me at all."

His brows rose in question.

"He said my mother was loved here, and the villagers were ready to accept her as one of their own, but something happened and that's why she left."

She held her breath, waiting for him to deny it, to cover it up.

"That's true."

He didn't miss a beat, didn't hesitate. Maybe this wasn't such a secret after all. "What happened to my mother here, Costa?"

He shuffled closer on the rock as if he wanted to reach for her hands, but she kept them locked under her thighs. "Are you sure you want to know everything?" he asked, "I asked my father some questions last night and suddenly everything made so much more sense."

Biting her lip, she nodded for him to go on.

"Your mother lost the love of her life here."

A pulse beat, thrum, thrum, thrum at her throat. "What do you mean 'the love of her life'?" Confusion hijacked her thoughts.

"I can understand why I didn't know the whole story—I was only a boy when she left—but didn't she tell you any of this?" he asked, as if he couldn't believe it was all new to her. "*Nothing?*"

"No, Costa, she told me nothing. None of this makes any sense." Hidden under her thighs, the pads of her fingers pressed into the rock beneath. Anchoring her.

"Your mother fell in love with a local man. It happened soon after she arrived on the island, and by all accounts they were inseparable."

Summer shrugged. "So, she had a relationship. A summer romance. Mom had many of those throughout her life, and she seemed happy with that."

He moved to the edge of the stone, his long legs hitting the ground, and then he held out his hands for hers. She slipped her hands into his and he held tight. Now she was anchored to Costa. "Your mother was in love, Summer. My father says she was engaged to be married."

Her instinctive reaction was to pull away, but he held her fast.

"There was a ceremony, an exchanging of rings. In the eyes of the Greek church, they'd embarked on the process of marriage and all the preparations for the wedding ceremony had begun."

Thoughts battered her mind. "Then why did she leave? Why didn't she—"

"There was an accident. After the engagement. Michali and his parents, Maria and Stavros, were killed in a car accident."

She wanted to get up, but couldn't, her plastered leg an anchor for her shaking body. "The house—?"

"**Dad says** Michali had bought this house for them to live in and it passed to your mother when he died."

For a second, Summer couldn't breathe. All the air had been sucked from her lungs.

Michali, the name the old woman had spoken at the wedding. The Michali that was gone, gone, gone. And the ring in the box, the gold band she'd asked Costa to sell. Her heart sank at the memory and turned cold.

"But why did she never tell me, Costa? She didn't know whether to be heartbroken or outraged. Why would her mother have kept something so important a secret?

She looked up into Costa's eyes. "Do you know how much this hurts? To know my mother had such a secret that she didn't want to share with me is—" A tear began to form and she stopped speaking as it grew fatter and finally spilled over and tracked its way down her cheek.

"Maybe she kept her life here a secret because she felt it was better to leave the past in the past." He lowered his voice and the emotion in it, the concern and the caring almost undid her. "Perhaps she knew she'd never find a love like she had with Michali, and that if you knew about it, you might feel like you were a mistake, an afterthought."

"But it answers so many questions I had about her: why

she never seemed interested in finding someone to be with, why she never talked about her life before she had me. If I'd only known some of this, I might not have been so—"

"Honest?" Costa gently shook both her hands, until she looked up at him. "You're right that you'll never know why she didn't tell you about Michali. Maybe it was all too painful, knowing what she could have had. Knowing what she lost."

Summer dragged her hands free, picked up her crutches and struggled to get them under her arms. "But don't you see. If Michali hadn't died, her life would have been so different. She wouldn't have been a traveler. She'd have had security, a home. She wouldn't have had..."

"You."

"Me, or money worries, or the responsibility of being a single mother in a judgmental world." She made her way into the house, desperate to get away so he couldn't see how upset she was, see her sadness and the raw emotion she knew was etched on her face.

Costa spoke as he followed her inside. "Who judged your mother, Summer?"

He said the exact words that were playing over and over in her own head. As she reached a window and looked sightlessly at the orchard, she whispered, "I did, Costa." And then even more softly. "I did."

"But you didn't know any of this," he said. "How could you?

Putting both palms to her cheeks, she softly rubbed away tears. "Don't you see, Costa? My whole impression of my mother was wrong. For good or bad, I made assumptions about her that weren't true. I can't rewrite history, I can only make my own, and when I sell this house and get on a plane back to reality, then I can begin living."

He took a step closer, near enough to touch her and her breath hitched in her throat.

"Why can't *this* be real, Summer—what's happening to you, to us, here and now? I don't want you to leave."

Something on his face had changed. His eyes were soft and his face open and shining.

"What...why..?"

"I'm in love with you."

The words were so unexpected, she reeled back in shock. "Me? You're in love with me?" Image after image of him with couture-clad women raged through her head. "You can't be... I don't... I'm not.."

He reached out a hand to touch her face. For a moment she thought her legs might give way, and she leaned more heavily on the crutch. As his fingers brushed the skin of her cheek, she knew for a fleeting second what it must have been like for her mother, being in love right here in this house on the other side of the world. Ever so briefly, everything seemed in harmony, not just the needs of her body satisfied, but for an instant the hole in her heart that she'd been carrying around since her mom died seemed filled.

Was this all it took? A belief that everything would turn out all right in the end? That something as simple as a leap of faith might be all it took to live in this forever?

Costa stepped closer and held her face in his warm, powerful hands, forcing her to look into his deep, dark eyes. Slowly, he bent his head and every cell in her body stretched to be closer to him, and when his lips touched hers in his commanding and confident way, she let herself succumb to the desire threading through her veins.

His kiss deepened and she let herself be swept along by the hopes and wishes that had been buried within her during the last three weeks. Lips moving together, the bliss of being so close filled her. Could he really love her? Could she have a life with him where all her fears were silenced, a life in which they could grow old and have a future that was so cruelly denied to her mother and *her* one true love?

Her body yielded to Costa's, her fingers buried in his sleek hair, her chest pressed close to his. His heartbeat strong and steady. Yes, it all seemed possible...until in one moment of clarity she realized it could never happen.

Slowly she pushed him away, but felt his resistance as he tried to keep her close. "Costa, no."

He still held her, although now his hands had slipped to her elbows. "I know you feel the same way, Summer. You have every right to be confused because of the secrets your mother and then I kept, but we can work things out. When you see that your mom only had your best interests at heart, and that I was upholding those things for her...then we'll be able to move beyond it."

She took a step back.

"I'll do whatever it takes to show you my love for you is real and something I'll never jeopardize again."

She took an extra deep breath to give her the strength, and although her heart raced, kept her voice steady. "Of course I have feelings for you, Costa." He stepped forward again, but she reached to the side and dragged a chair closer so she could lean on it. "But that's where it has to end."

"Why?" His voice was calm, but his eyes held a power she hadn't seen before.

"Because you can't offer what I need." Suddenly her leg was a dead weight, and she sank onto the chair.

Costa blew out a scant breath, then pulled up another chair, so close Summer wriggled back a little so she wouldn't be tempted to reach out to him.

"Summer, I can give you *everything*. I have houses in three countries, businesses that can support us so you never need to work if you don't want to. We can travel the world collecting every ornament you lay eyes on. Hell, Summer, I can take you to the finest bazaars in Istanbul where you can choose a *room* full of carpets." His eyes were wide and imploring, and she realized with a sinking heart that he hadn't understood what she'd meant.

She placed the crutches on the floor and leaned forward a little. The last thing she wanted to do was hurt him or herself. "It's no surprise you and my mother maintained such a strong relationship," she said softly. "In essence, you were so very much alike."

He smiled, and it sailed straight into her soul, making this so much harder. "Because she taught me about being the best you can be."

"Yes, but also because you're both travelers. You want to explore the world, Costa, live from day to day without roots or links to your past. You've mentioned it nearly every time we've spoken about our lives. In that way, you are so very much like my mother, but it's a life I don't want to live.

"From the day I was born I've been moved, here and there, backward and forward, and it's not enough for me. I want to go home to Brentwood Bay, where people know me, care about me." She swallowed back the wobble in her words. How could she be doing this to beautiful, thoughtful, Costa? The man who'd given up a month of his life to fulfill a promise to someone he held dear. Because there was one overriding reason she *could* do this and *would* do this. "I want to give my children the gift of a stable life where they learn to value the community they're a part of."

"But that community can be anywhere," Costa said, his eyes sparking. "Surely the most important thing is *love*."

The word sliced into Summer's body and she sat a little taller to deflect its power. No matter how much she wished it to be true, she knew in her deepest heart that although Costa might love her *now*, he couldn't offer her the thing she most deeply craved—security.

"The swallows," she said, not wanting to pass judgment on the way he'd chosen to live his life, but searching for a way to make him understand. "They don't truly belong anywhere. In spring, they come back here because it's instinctual. They're drawn here, but look at the trouble they have to go through—redefining what's been here before, mending, rebuilding—and all for what...so they can leave it all and fly to Africa before winter, just to repeat the process all over again?"

She stopped, wondering if she was being too simplistic. "You've taught me so much," she said, her voice wobbling with emotion she didn't want to hide, "but we're too different, Costa. Don't you see? I don't want to...I just can't live like that."

His features darkened, and anger flashed in his eyes. "Have you learned nothing from being here?" he said sharply. "Can't you see that your mother was robbed of exactly what you and I have, what we can build Summer? Don't you see that we have the opportunity to have what she spent the rest of her life searching for?"

Summer squirmed in her chair as the small hairs on the back of her neck stood to attention. Was he right? Should she be giving him up for things as simple as stability and permanence?

He stood, and she was reminded of his size, his power in all parts of his life. "I don't know what lessons your mother had in mind when she brought me back to this island. Maybe she wanted me to evaluate what I'd become, maybe she wanted me to heal my relationship with my father. But there's one thing I *do* know—I've found you and you've found me. I won't give you up for something that can be so easily fixed."

She stayed silent and thought about everything her mother had lost. *The love of her life*.

"Your swallows may travel, migrate, build homes in different places..." The air sparked with the strength of his words. "But they also mate for life."

Summer thrust both hands under her thighs to prevent them being slammed over her ears. She didn't need any more guilt, didn't want to choose between him and the life she'd always wanted. He needed to admit to himself that this was completely impossible, so she raised her voice. "Could *you* give it all up?

"What?" His voice was gruff.

"The traveling, the moving from place to place? Could you see yourself becoming part of a community where the greatest concern was when to hold the village fete?"

He didn't answer, so she continued, but this time her voice was tender. "I could *never* ask you to do those things because we have different values.. Maybe it's because you had them as a child and don't feel a need to have them in your life now, but I do. And asking you to give them up is the same as asking me to give up my idea of stability and community."

Still, he said nothing, just stood with his head held high and his gaze fixed on hers.

Summer hurried on, wanting to stay close but knowing she had to push him away. "You mean so much to me, Costa. I can't thank you enough for everything you've done and we've had some wonderful times together, but as I said before, our lives are opposite, our needs are so different."

Finally he spoke, his words short and hard. "There is only one thing *I* need, Summer, and it's you."

"I'm sorry," Costa, she said, the words catching in her throat. "I'm really, really sorry but it's over."

CHAPTER THIRTEEN

*C*osta signed the last of the real estate documents, handed them back to the agent, and strode out into the afternoon sun. He'd bought the house in the name of one of his local charities so Summer wouldn't recognize the buyer. Not that she'd be able to decipher the Greek script, anyway.

The community would decide how they wanted to use it —perhaps accommodation for visiting students, or a home for a family in need. But whatever it was eventually used for, Costa was sure Caroline would have approved. Technically, *he* wouldn't be giving Summer any money in the transaction. She'd done the main part of what her mother had wanted for her—seen the project through—and now she could leave and return to the life she yearned for.

Leave.

The word hammered in his brain. He'd listened to what she'd said about his lifestyle, his priorities, and every word was true. What *could* he offer her?

This sale and the dissolution of their marriage were the only things he could do to give Summer her freedom. He'd had the dissolution papers drawn up and his lawyer would forward them to her.

She'd made it clear she didn't want a future with him.

His chest tightened as he remembered the way their eyes had locked when she'd asked him to leave last night. He'd *always* got what he wanted, *always* had the last say.

Not this time.

With a shake of his head, he realized he'd fulfilled the dream Caroline had had for him—to return home and appreciate what had always been a part of him—but she couldn't have imagined the price he would pay.

At least Summer had grown to know her mother in the last three weeks and would leave here with the life she wanted. But damn it, why couldn't that life be with him?

He reached into his pocket and pulled out Caroline's gold engagement band, which he'd collected from the jeweler's safekeeping. He turned the delicate ring in his fingers. Could he bear the pain of seeing Summer again before she left? Maybe he could ask someone else to give it to her? They'd watch her slip it on her finger as he'd imagined doing a hundred times, see the way her face lit up...

The estate agent had told him she wanted to leave on the earliest boat possible, which could be tonight.

As he strode down the hill to his father's house, Costa thought back to the day the whole school, in fact almost the entire village, had gone down to the dock to wave Caroline goodbye. He remembered some of the old women, tears streaming down their creased faces as they pleaded with her to stay while she moved down the line and hugged them all. He'd never truly known why Caroline had left, why she couldn't stay, but now he guessed it was because part of her heart had died here.

∾

Summer brushed away a rogue tear as she folded the last of her clothes and placed them in the battered suitcase sitting amongst the crumpled linen on her bed.

Tossed on the nightstand was the contract for the sale of the house she'd signed the night before when the real estate agent had arrived unexpectedly at her door. Of course, she couldn't read the documents in Greek, and should probably have asked Costa to look over them, but after his hasty exit she felt it would be unfair to ask him to do any more for her. She wasn't even sure if he'd slept downstairs last night.

Tears again pushed their way across her vision and she blinked them rapidly away, ignoring the accompanying ache in her chest. Count her blessings—that's what she'd do. There were a million reasons why she should be happy right now, but her frozen heart overwhelmed them all.

This house was sold, and there was enough money to close on her dream home in Brentwood Bay. Against the odds and a broken leg, she'd renovated her mother's house, transformed it from a run-down uninhabitable shack to a gorgeous villa. Not many twenty-somethings could boast such a house renovation on a Greek island.

Most importantly, she'd made peace with her mom. Reaching for the *tiki* at her throat, she realized that although it still hurt that her mom hadn't shared such a major part of her life with her, she knew deep down that some of her mother's motivation for sending her here had been to learn about herself.

Her desire for a home was no longer born from hurt at the way her mother had lived her life. Now she knew the truth, Summer wanted to honor what her mother had lost by being true to herself. Just as Caroline had done.

There was no need for her to linger. The buyer was keen to take possession as soon as possible. Athina and Socrates had finished their lessons, and Summer had lost any chance of a life with a man who stopped her heart when he walked in the room and made her feel like the only other person in the world.

When she'd watched him stride up the hill from her house last night, she'd managed to hold in the tears, her chest heaving until he was out of sight, but then she'd collapsed and lay huddled in a frozen ball till she was roused by the estate agent.

Would she see Costa again? Her head said no, but her heart willed it. Their marriage needed to be dissolved, and she'd face that when she was home, when the vision of him didn't dance relentlessly in her mind.

With no reason to stay, she'd booked herself on the first ferry to Athens the next morning.

After placing the last of her clothes in the case, Summer shut the lid and surveyed the room. The toes on her bare foot sunk into the rich pile of the rug and she briefly wondered who would live here next.

Who would light the fire in the grate and listen for the *koulouri* man? Who would go down to the orchard and pick the blood oranges for the most delicious juice? Who would look out for the swallows in their special little home in her roof?

Again, she felt the ache of tears behind her eyes and for now she let them fall. One last time, if she could manage it, she'd climb the ladder and check on her birds before packing the rest of her things—the coffee pots, the turquoise bowl...

After picking up some *koulouri* left over from her break-fast, Summer let herself out the back door and breathed in the familiar tang of wild oregano and oranges. Perhaps when she got back to Brentwood Bay, she could plant some of the herb in a pot to sit at her back door just like...

No. It wouldn't be the same at all.

She placed the ladder against the side of the house.

Maybe she could put her good leg on a rung and drag herself up with her arms? For a second she had an image of Costa holding her in *his* arms when she'd fallen, the strength of his chest, the thud of his heart as he'd carried her up the hill, the touch of his lips as he'd pressed a kiss to her forehead...

Looking up, she placed one foot on the bottom rung before she lurched back as a voice yelled, "Are you kidding me?!"

Costa was at her side before she had a chance to prepare how she would react, and then the familiar rush of adrenaline left her momentarily weak.

"Do you have a death wish?" he asked gruffly, dragging the ladder toward him. "I don't know how on earth you thought you'd get up there with a broken foot."

Summer blinked, wishing his eyes weren't hidden behind dark glasses so she could read his emotions.

Sticking her chin out, she said, "I wanted to check on my birds before I leave."

"You're leaving?" He didn't sound surprised.

"On the early morning boat tomorrow. The house has been sold, so there's no need for me to stay any longer."

He didn't respond, but he put the ladder against the wall again and started to climb.

"Would you mind putting this in there?" Summer asked, trying to keep her voice even as she held the piece of bread between her fingers.

He hesitated for a moment, then came back down and reached for the bread. As his hand brushed hers, Summer took an involuntary breath and let the feel of him sink to her core.

He didn't react to her touch and proceeded to climb. When he reached the roofline, she waited while he removed a tile before she asked nervously, "What do you see?"

He hesitated for a moment, dragging a hand through his hair. Then he dropped the bread in.

"Are they there? Are they okay?"

He placed the tile back on the roof and began his descent.

"Costa?"

"She's sitting on eggs."

For one ridiculous moment, Summer felt the grin that swept across her face. The birds had come back. Despite the fright and upheaval of the renovations and her attempt at moving the nest, they'd rebuilt their home and were creating a family.

The irony wasn't lost on her, and the grin slipped from her face when Costa reached the ground and turned to her.

"So, you're really going?" Summer held her forearms in a half-hug in the same line of defense he'd seen the first day they'd met, her beautiful face tilted to him.

"Yes, the estate agent found a buyer. Some community trust, and they want to take possession as soon as possible, so I'm free to go. The agent said the money would be in my account by the end of the week." She spoke quickly, her words running into each other. "Apart from getting my plaster off and a temporary splint put on this afternoon, there's nothing else I need to do here."

Reach out, touch her, tell her it can't end this way. Voices, loud and belligerent, chanted in his head. She carried on talking, but he heard nothing as his gaze focused on the pink of her lips, the arch of her neck, parts of her he couldn't bear to think of not touching again.

"Costa?"

"I'm sorry?"

"I asked when you'll be leaving?"

He looked away then, across to the grassy bank on the other side of the orchard. He could hear the resolution in her voice, the determination to leave and get back to her life. Jamming his hands in his pockets, his fingers found the ring, and he squeezed.

"In the next few days," he said briskly. "I have some things to complete for my father before I go."

"So things are better with him?"

"Yes." Why couldn't he tell her that meeting her had changed his life completely? That he could never have imagined a time when he would enjoy talking with his father as he had in the last few days, sitting in the *kafenion* and discussing life with the men of the village.

Because he had to let her go, had to give her up so she could live the dream she'd always had of stability and constancy.

"Will you come and say goodbye?" Her voice was quiet, and when he didn't look down at her, she reached out a hand and touched his arm. "At the boat, I mean. Will you come and see me off?"

He willed her hand to stay there, for the warmth of its imprint to stay part of him for a lifetime, but it had to end.

He placed his hands behind his back, causing her hand to drop. If he couldn't give her the ring the way he'd imagined, if he couldn't drag her into his arms the way his body demanded, then this had to be it. "No, Summer, I won't."

"Why not?"

Her voice caught. He could hear the tremble, so he pushed his glasses up on his head so she could see his eyes and not doubt her decision. She didn't need to question herself, didn't need to deal with his emotion as well. "Because I want to remember you here, in this house we completed together." He swallowed. "I've told you how I feel and that will never change, but I want you to also know that I admire you."

Her head bowed and her eyelids fluttered closed as if she were steeling herself against his words.

"You've met your mother's challenge, and although you were upset about how she did it, you've maintained your dignity and your goals, and I deeply respect that."

Her chest moved as she took a deep breath. He needed to let her go, let her live the life she had chosen. He reached out and touched both her elbows, then waited until she looked up at him. "I love you, Summer, and I always will, but you need to live your life and I need to live mine."

As he spoke, her eyes opened and her lips parted. As her whole body moved toward him and she stretched up on tiptoe, he knew she wanted to be kissed, knew she wanted to touch him one more time—but it was too much. With all the strength he could muster, Costa turned and walked away.

CHAPTER FOURTEEN

*S*ummer wasn't quite sure how she managed to get down to the dock in one piece the next morning. The tears had barely stopped since Costa's departure the day before, and every goodbye she'd said since had made things worse. Going to the *kafenion* in the late afternoon had been especially hard yesterday, as she'd said goodbye to Yianni, Socrates and Takis, then to Athina and many of her neighbors on the way back home.

They'd all begged her to stay; Athina had dissolved in tears. Yianni and Takis had both held her hands in a vicelike grip until she'd had to pull hers away. Their sorrowful eyes and hopeful faces had momentarily confused her until reality hit home.

She'd had to constantly remind herself why she was leaving, that staying here without Costa would be too hard to bear— perhaps the sort of decision her mother had come to when she'd lost Michali.

As she sat on the old wooden dock and waited for the ferry that would take her back to Athens, she held a hand above her eyes and looked up at the village as it seemed to tumble down from the hilltop. The aged white stone of the houses against the iridescent blue of the morning sky took her breath away.

Costa was up there somewhere, probably packing to leave. Her heart ached to see him one more time, to feel the strength of him as he pulled her into an all-consuming embrace.

She knew why he'd had to leave yesterday; it was finished, there was nothing more to say, but it hadn't stopped her feeling bereft. Letting her hand drop, the tinkle of the pink beads around her wrist pulled her thoughts back to the house.

One of the last things she'd done before leaving was to get Socrates to haul the wooden box back up the ladder into the space in the ceiling. It didn't seem right to remove the picture of her mother and Michali from its final resting place. Her heart ached at the thought of the engagement ring she'd asked Costa to sell, but at least she could take the beads with her. She'd formed them into a double strand, and they would now lie close to her skin—always.

Turning again to look out to sea, her heart dropped like a stone as she saw the ferry rounding the point in the distance. Within the hour she'd be on board, heading back to a life on the other side of the world, and it felt all wrong.

Her head swung back to the vista of the village, and her gaze drank in the view one more time, etching it into her memory. An old man watered pots of something green on his balcony. A woman was beating dust from a mat as it hung over a wall. Then Summer's gaze was drawn to a line of movement at the top of the hill.

Three or four people were moving at quite a pace down the labyrinth of paths, and as they passed houses, more people seemed to be joining them. The figure at the front seemed to be moving particularly swiftly, and everyone else was hurrying to keep pace. Perhaps they were meeting someone from the boat.

Summer put a hand across her forehead again to shade her eyes from the bright sun as she looked closer, and her heart began to beat harder in her chest.

Was it? Could it be?

The line grew longer as people joined from every house that was passed. She could hear the buzz of excited conversation now as voices carried down to the dock on the sea breeze. Summer stood, aware of the thump of her heart against her chest wall. The gait, the confident stride, she'd watched that body so many times, knew it so intimately, it left her in no doubt who was leading this procession.

Her hand covered her mouth in panic. He wouldn't do it, would he? Try to convince her to be with him, to fly away to his life, wherever that might be? And he wouldn't use the villagers to help him, would he? Swinging around to check the progress of the ferry, she was momentarily relieved it was still some distance away.

At least she could say goodbye one final time.

The crowd was only a few feet away now, but they were a blur as all Summer could focus on was Costa. His hair, usually so sleek and in place, was windblown, and the color of his cheeks was a deep tan from his days spent working outdoors on the house.

Steeling herself for his persuasive speech, Summer stood straighter, but butterflies danced in her stomach. The crowd stopped, but Costa kept walking, all the while a smile growing broader across his face. Their gazes locked, and Summer drew in a breath at the stunning sight of him. Every few seconds she expected him to stop, to stand straight and tall and start speaking, but he just strode closer and closer until suddenly she was in his arms and his lips, firm, full and hard were on hers.

All sound left her ears. All sight left her eyes. Every one of her senses converged in the depth of this kiss. Aware of nothing but her connection with the man who made her heart soar, Summer let herself drown in him. Warmth moved from her lips, across her neck and down her spine as she pulled his body even closer. Only when his hands touched her face and he gently pulled her away did she see the beaming smile lighting up his features.

With sparkling eyes, he spoke. "Thank God you're still here. I thought I'd lost you. Summer, you can't go, you mustn't leave, this isn't right."

Stepping back so his hands fell from her face, she whispered, "Please don't."

A frown crossed his forehead before he continued. "But you don't understand. I'm staying." He took a step to the side then, and she became aware of the crowd behind him. "This is what you've done for me, Summer." He swept both arms wide to indicate the people. "This is what I should have realized days ago, but it wasn't until I saw how determined you were to live your dream that I realized it was what I wanted too."

The old woman, Michali's aunt, stepped forward and shooed the villagers back so they could have more privacy, and Costa stepped closer again.

"I understand what you want, Summer. Stability and certainty and a community you can become part of and grow in. Well, those things are all here for you, and as I've discovered, they're here for me too."

The edge of excitement in his voice was lost as he spoke more quietly. "I know why your mother wanted me to return here, Summer. It was so I could come back to the sort of life *she* would have had if it hadn't been stolen from her. I was up all night talking with my father. Something I haven't done in years. I'm going to take up my birthright. I'm going to lead all these wonderful people and stand ...for mayor." He paused as if to gauge her reaction, then continued. "With you by my side."

Tears began to push their way into Summer's eyes, but she bit her lip in an attempt to stop them.

"And I've realized why your mother sent you back here too."

Still she couldn't speak.

"Your mother sent you back to the place where she felt safest, to a place that was home. Your mother wanted you to experience what she had."

Costa stepped closer and touched her shoulders. "Remember the photo of your mother and Michali?"

Summer nodded.

"Your mother left that photo here because it didn't belong anywhere else. She knew she couldn't take what she had with Michali and transport it to somewhere else, with someone else. Your mother *had* to leave here Summer, but you don't. You have the ability to live the sort of life she would have had if she'd had the chance."

Finally, Summer found her voice. "But why do you want to stay here? Why now?" She wouldn't let herself imagine this could be real until she heard him speak the words.

"I came to a decision that this is where I want to spend my life, in the company of people who know me, care about me and who I can learn to be a part of again. I've achieved many things on my own, things I'm extremely proud of. But the time has come for me to become part of my community, to be who I am, who I've always been."

The horn from the approaching ferry sounded long and low, and they both turned to look out to sea.

When she turned back to look at Costa, Summer spoke quietly. "And if I say I'm still leaving?"

He hesitated for just a moment, then looked deeper into

her eyes. "Then I'll have lost the love of my life, as your mother did, but just like her, I'll go on doing what I need to do, doing the things that make me happy, right here where I belong."

Knowing those were the words she needed to hear, Summer launched herself into his arms. "And we can have a house and a fireplace and a couple of swallows in the ceiling?"

He didn't answer as he rained kisses across her face.

"And an orange grove and rice pudding for breakfast?" Summer knew in the deepest part of her that she loved Costa.

The kisses stopped, and Costa tilted her chin so she looked up at him. "And carpets on the floor and ornaments on the wall."

Summer began to laugh and cry at the same time, tears blurring her vision until Costa wiped them away and took her hand. "There is one more thing," he said quietly before turning his back to her and showing something to the crowd. "Something I should have done properly the first time."

Whoops of encouragement and laughter rang around the dock.

He turned back to her and opened his fist. Summer gasped as she saw her mother's ring. "You didn't sell it!" she cried, the tears beginning afresh. "I thought it was lost forever!"

Costa took hold of her hand and gently slipped the ring on her trembling finger, then leaned closer to whisper in her ear, "And I thought *we* were lost forever."

Summer looked up into his shining charcoal eyes. "I love you, Costa. And we can't be lost when we've both just found home."

***

Thank you so much for reading *A Home for Summer*. I hope you love Summer and Costa as much as I do.

Find out what's happening now with the Katsalos family in the fifth book in the series *A Marriage for Show - Christo's story* available as an e book on Amazon, or ask for it at your local book store or library.

And to find out about new books, sign up for my newsletter **here or email** barb@barbaradeleo.com. When you sign up I'll send you the FREE prequel to this series *Waiting on Forever - Alex's story*!

If you love the people of Brentwood Bay, meet more of them in the *Breaking Through* series! You can find Book 1 *Bad Reputations* as an e book on Amazon, or ask for it at your local book store or library.

I hugely appreciate your help in spreading the word about my books, including telling a friend. Reviews help readers find books! Please review *A Home for Summer* **here** or on your favorite site.

Turn the page for an excerpt from *A Marriage for Show-Christo's story*.

NEXT UP IN THE TALL, DARK AND
DRIVEN SERIES...

A Marriage for Show

Christo's story

Property tycoon Christo Mantazis wants the one thing his riches can't buy—the villa where his mother has lived and worked as housekeeper for forty years. That it's the same house he was banished from after being caught making love to the owner's irresistible daughter stirs up old memories, and now he wants her more than ever.

Magazine editor Ruby Fleming's not about to give up her home to Christo, the man who broke her heart—until she discovers her mother left half of the estate to him, and she realizes she's trapped. When Christo offers a marriage of convenience, Ruby knows it's the only way for them to get what they want. Ruby needs a link to her past, and Christo needs his mother to retain her home.

But it's another need—to have Christo again—that Ruby must resist at all costs.

You can read the first chapter of *A Marriage for Show - Christo's story* on the next few pages.

You can buy *A Marriage for Show* here or ask for it at your local book store or library.

A MARRIAGE FOR SHOW
CHAPTER ONE

A kaleidoscope of color sparkled overhead as Ruby Fleming kicked toward the surface of her late parents' Olympic-sized swimming pool. The cool water across her skin was a relief from the sticky heat of a Brentwood Bay evening and the heart-wrenching turmoil of the last few weeks. It seemed too cruel to be real that the precious life inside her had lost both a father and grandmother in the space of a month.

Ruby broke through the surface, tossed her long hair over her shoulder, and flicked water from her eyes. When she'd got her breath back and focused, her heart constricted in her chest as she froze. An imposing figure stood shadowed by the wisteria-covered terrace above the pool, a selection of designer luggage at his feet.

Dread crawled the length of her spine. The last of the mourners had left in the days after her mother's funeral, and Stella the housekeeper hadn't been here when Ruby had arrived in such a hurry from New York. She *should* be the only person on the estate.

This six-foot plus package of sizzling masculinity made a lie of that.

Her heart beat harder as she waded in shoulder-deep water to the pool's tiled edge. How long had he been standing there, watching her, waiting?

Razor-edged suit. Vanilla crème shirt against mocha skin. A stance of unleashed determination. Her stomach somersaulted as she blinked and then frowned. There was something familiar...

The man stepped forward, the classic angles of his face grim, and the sense of familiarity burned deeper.

"My condolences for the loss of your mother. She was a very generous and caring woman. She'll be missed."

The words, like tumbling river stones, washed over her in a wave of realization. His voice was more mature than she remembered, but its sensuality, the way it sang in her ears and rocketed straight to her core, was the same as ten years ago.

"Christo."

She swallowed away his name as her pulse sprinted. The month-long scar of tears and regret she wore like a brand bit deep. "I'm sorry you couldn't get here sooner. The funeral was Friday."

As he moved closer, the dark cloud stamped across his face shifted a fraction, and on reflex, Ruby splayed the fingers of both hands across her bare belly beneath the water —holding herself together, keeping every part of her private.

She hadn't seen Christo Mantazis in a decade, but knew being around him caused her to lose focus on what was right, what was important. And nothing was more important than this baby.

He'd been nineteen then, when he'd moved out of the quarters he shared with his mother, Stella, the estate's housekeeper.

No longer having an impressive street address or influential people to mix with, he'd tried to stay connected with Ruby's privileged world by bedding her. Only when her father caught them and confronted him did Christo back away. Fast. He'd also been seen with other women at the polo club and the yacht club, trying to make connections that would stick.

She'd asked Christo one question on the day her father had banished him from the estate and her life—did he want her or the package she came with? He'd left the house without giving her an answer. Without fighting for their relationship. Without fighting for *her*. And he'd taken a precious part of her heart with him.

"I've come from the airport." His voice lowered and took on a harder edge. "We were in Greece when we heard."

We. Did he mean himself and his mother?

Ruby craned her neck, searching, and kept her voice steady when she asked, "Is Stella with you?"

"Mother is back at my apartment. She's upset about Antonia's death, especially distraught that the funeral was held so quickly. I've brought my aunt from Greece to stay with her until matters are finalized."

Ruby dipped her shoulders lower, glad for the cool water on her overheated skin. Seeing Christo again unsettled her more than she'd ever imagined, particularly when he was talking in riddles.

"Which matters?"

He dragged gold-rimmed aviator glasses from his face, and her breath hitched as his onyx gaze pinned hers. Glossy black hair licked the burnished skin of his face and framed a masculine jaw darkened by the shadow of travel-induced stubble. His lips, lips she'd once hungered for, were set in a rigid line. Ten years might've passed, but he was as striking...no, more striking than she remembered.

He tapped the sunglasses against a thigh standing taut

under the fine suit fabric. Memories of being tangled in his arms ripped through her, and her stomach looped. She bit her lip. God help her, she hoped he wasn't staying long.

He reached for his jacket's inside pocket and withdrew a white envelope.

"This contains a bank check for an amount to cover my purchase of your share of this property." His voice cut through her, face impassive. "In a perfect world, I wouldn't intrude on your grief so soon, but I've no choice. My offer's more than generous."

Ruby blinked. Her *share* of this property? She was an only child. Her mother didn't have anyone else to leave the house to. She touched her palm to her belly—well, no one her mother had known about.

Trying to clear her mind, she shook her hair and water droplets rained on the surface of the pool. "What offer?"

He bent and scooped up the large red towel at his feet and held it open invitingly. "Come out of the water and we'll discuss it." The power of his look and the cold, detached tone didn't match the broad expanse of his open arms.

Ruby's blood chilled and she clutched her body tighter. "I'm fine where I am, thank you." She wasn't moving from the privacy of the water. He didn't need to see more of her ripening body than he already had. "Tell me, Christo, what offer?"

He stood silent for a moment, then tossed the towel and envelope on the ornate iron table. He pulled up a chair before effortlessly folding his six-plus frame into it. Drumming his fingers on the tabletop, he lifted his chin and fixed her with a firm stare.

"You return to New York when?"

The early evening breeze shuffled leaves at the corner of the tennis court, and despite the heat of the day, Ruby shivered. He'd avoided her question and his tone was rough, careless—so different from the secret, sensual way he'd spoken to her in the past. Whispering of his desire for her, words she'd foolishly believed. She looked down and swallowed past the lump in her throat. Her world had been turned on its head in the last month, nothing was clear anymore.

In a matter of weeks she'd learned of her pregnancy and that the father—a man she'd dated briefly—had died in a car wreck. Now her mother, who she hadn't seen in years, was gone and it was as if she were being pulled into some frightening black hole. And here was Christo, a shock in itself, using phrases like "share of this property."

Christo had changed. The fiercely passionate boy was now an intense man who radiated heat and raw energy, and something wild and pulsing strained beneath his surface. Something that caused a glow to burn through her body every time he looked at her.

He'd asked when she was returning to New York. She lifted her chin.

It was none of his business.

"I'm not making any big decisions right now."

"You wouldn't come back here to live." The bold certainty in his statement stung. "You haven't been back since you were a child."

A child? She gripped the frigid edge of the pool. He'd thought of her as a child back then? She'd been a young adult, and there had been nothing childlike in the way she'd felt about him. And nothing innocent in the inexcusable way he'd treated her. Leaving without an explanation. Never contacting her again.

Eighteen and ecstatically happy in his arms, it had devastated her when her father had confronted him with the truth of his womanizing and banished Christo from the house. When she'd angrily gone after him to explain how much he'd hurt her, Christo had turned the anger back on her, asking why she hadn't stood up for him. Couldn't he see that he'd broken the trust she'd so carefully placed in him? Taken her from the heights of sizzling passion to the depths of confusion? If her father's allegations weren't true, then Christo would've stayed and fought for her. Not walked out of her life. Of that, she was certain.

The double hurt that had bored through her all those years ago leaked into her words. "I've been back." She scanned his inscrutable face. *When you were on your annual trip to Greece*. In truth, returning to Brentwood Bay on those few occasions had been difficult, hurtful. Leaving her home town because she couldn't live with the secret of her mother's long-term affair—and the broken family it had caused—had seemed her only option then, but in recent years she'd yearned for a sense of her old self, her heritage.

Being away for most of a decade had meant she'd managed to avoid Christo. Whenever his name was mentioned when she was back, she'd tried to blank out the details. He hadn't been here since her father had told him all those years ago to never come back, and he had no business being here now.

She asked again. "What *offer*, Christo?"

Dark shadows passed across his chiseled features, and he leaned back in the chair, scrutinizing her. "Antonia didn't discuss her will? She told you nothing of her plans?"

Her heart drummed in her chest. Surely he knew that she and her mother hadn't been close. "No, she didn't. Her death was so sudden—her heart problem had been undetected. Her lawyer has asked to see me tomorrow to discuss her wishes. I'm sure everything will be in order." A stab deep in her throat reminded her how little she'd known of her mother in the last few years. Forgiveness for the pain her mother had caused their family with her affair hadn't come easily to

Ruby. Now she'd never have the chance to tell her mother she'd loved her despite the past. She blinked that tragedy away.

She scanned Christo's face, the dark lashes that framed his unforgiving stare, and she swallowed. Why was he mentioning estates and offers when it was *her* mother who'd been buried this week? "Tell me what you know, Christo."

"You and I are joint beneficiaries of the major part of your mother's estate. This property." His jaw set firmer. "I'm here to buy you out."

For a moment, the water around her seemed to move before she realized it was her body that was swaying. She grabbed hold of the tiled edge to steady herself, his words pulsing in her head. They didn't make sense. None of this did. "You can't... she wouldn't..."

In a second he was on his feet, his sleeve pushed up, holding out a strong hand to her.

"Ruby, take my hand." She stared at his broad, welcoming palm and tried to straighten everything in her mind, wanting someone to save her from this nightmare. Anyone but him.

He was to have a half share of this house? Her childhood home? The place that should pass to her child as it had to five generations of Flemings before?

No.

His voice deepened, commanded, "Ruby, get out of the pool."

Mindless, she put her hand in his and the second their skin connected, a bolt of heat flared through her, a connection so strong it stole the breath from her lungs. With frightening speed, he lifted her out until she stood dripping on his beautifully polished shoes. As her cool hand warmed in his sure grip, she slowly looked up into his face and her throat closed.

Eyes the color of midnight sent a smoldering rope

throughout her body, and she dragged in a bigger breath as he surveyed her from top to toe. This wasn't happening. Couldn't be. He reached for the towel and placed it around her shoulders.

Grabbing the loose corners, she rushed to conceal the curve of her belly. "I don't believe you." Her voice was rough and raw. "My mother would never leave half the house to you after what you did. We might've had our difficulties, but she'd never want to hurt me."

Holding her steady, the strength in his hands burned through the towel, his polished, perfect male scent invading her senses. "You *will* believe it. The documentation is succinct and clear. You'll receive all the details from your mother's lawyer in time, but we'll resolve ownership now to keep things simple."

Ruby sank into the iron chair behind her, limbs loose, skin chilling. "Why would she do this? We hadn't spoken much lately, but I'd have thought that with something so significant..."

He took the chair opposite and leaned back, twilight causing the bronze of his skin to deepen and shadows to settle in the contours of his face. "So I could buy your share."

"You spoke to her about it in person?"

For the briefest moment, a soft change swept across his face before it vanished. "She was a complex but deeply caring woman. We spoke many times. She knew you had no interest in returning here to stay, so she wanted to offer you an easy exit. At the same time, she'd ensure the house went to someone who appreciated it."

With frozen fingers, Ruby pulled the towel tight across her body as his stare hardened once more. Her father had banished him, and Christo had been furious at her father's decree. The son of an immigrant housekeeper, he'd seen her as an open door into another, more privileged world. What on earth had persuaded her mother to leave this property to Christo Mantazis now? He'd obviously convinced her that either he'd made a mistake all those years ago or, by some miracle, he'd changed.

From the way he sat, inscrutable and closed but with his gaze skimming her body, Ruby believed neither. She raised her chin a fraction. "I can't think why she'd have wanted to provide for you, but why didn't she just give you money? Why a share of our house?"

With an ironic smile, he flicked his wrist and a designer watch jangled against the table. "It's not money I need, Ruby." His voice was smooth and self-assured.

The exquisite suit, the brand name luggage—he'd come a very long way in ten years. "Then, what?"

He leaned forward, a forearm resting on the table edge, and the crisp, clean scent of him surrounded her. "My mother has lived in this house for decades. It's the only home she's ever known in this country and the only place she'll be happy. You haven't lived here for years."

Her mind raced. Although she felt for Stella—losing a close friend and her job at the same time—Ruby couldn't possibly sell this house, her baby's birthright. This estate had been in her father's family for generations, and although it hadn't housed a happy family in a very long time, she intended to change that. In the last few years, something had been calling her. A yearning to put right the hurts of the past, to find the old self she'd fled from. Her mother's unexpected death had been a cruel blow to her search, but Christo wasn't going to stop that journey with his confident words and dollar bills.

The solution was simple. "I intend to keep the house, but Stella can stay, of course. It's so huge that there's always plenty to do here. I'll buy your half and everything can be settled."

His look hardened and the confidence oozing from him funneled through her. "As I said, I don't want your money. What I want is this house for my mother's retirement. Not a house for her to keep working in. I'll pay you three times its worth to see that happens. You can buy yourself a permanent place in New York and never feel tied to Brentwood Bay again."

Ruby sat straighter, her shoulders tightening. He was telling her what to do and where to live now? "I won't be selling my share, Christo. I grew up in this house, it's part of my heritage, and even though I haven't spent much time here recently, it's more important to me than you understand. Your mother can stay here without working for as long as she wants. God knows she deserves it after being such a wonderful companion to my mother. Whether I spend most of my time in New York or here, Stella will always be welcome in this house." Light relief danced through her chest as the idea blossomed. "Yes, I'd love to think of her here. It'll be perfect for both of us."

And my precious baby.

She put a hand to her trembling lips. There was a time Stella Mantazis had been like a second mother to her, and now that her own mother was gone, she couldn't think of anyone more perfect to share her house—or her baby—with.

"Not good enough." His stare held stark irritation. "Now's the time for my mother to be taken care of and cherished, not put up as some sort of charity case lodger. She'll live in this house as its owner, nothing less."

The weight of his determination and the events of the last few weeks drilled into her. Now was not the time to be having this discussion. "This house belongs to me and future generations of Flemings. It's where I'm going to stay." She stood.

"And where I'll stay, too."

Blood changed direction in her veins. "I beg your pardon?"

He moved from the chair and pushed himself to his full height, determination flaring across his features. "Your mother spoke of one condition in her will."

Her lips dried, but she forced the words out. "And what's that?"

"The first person to leave forfeits their share." He picked up a suitcase in each hand. "If you're staying, Ruby, then you can bet I'm staying too."

You can buy *A Marriage for Show* here or ask for it at your local book store or library.

GET A FREE NOVELLA

Throughout my career, my readers have been such a key part of my writing life, and I love to keep them up-to-date with what I'm doing. I occasionally send out newsletters with details on both new releases and extra special offers for my books and others like mine. I promise I won't bombard you!

If you sign up to my mailing list, the first thing I'll send you is a **FREE** novella, ***Waiting on Forever***, the prequel to my ***Tall, Dark and Driven*** series.

One last task to complete, then Alex Panos can fulfil a heart breaking promise. That is, if he can get past cute and quirky Mara Hemmingway.

On her own since she was sixteen, Mara won't be taken advantage of again—especially not by brooding and troubled Alex. Instead, she'll play him at his own game.

When their powerful attraction threatens to get in the way of both their dreams, someone will have to face a future of waiting on forever.

You can claim your **FREE** novella by clicking here or emailing barb@barbaradeleo.com!

LOVE BARBARA'S BOOKS?

If you really enjoyed *A Home for Summer* and fancy reading a lot more about the crazy, lovable Katsalos family, as well as Barbara's next series, apply to join Barbara's review team!

Barbara is now taking applications to join her Advanced Review team. If you're selected, you'll get all of Barbara's releases free, up to a month before release!

Fill out an application here or mail barb@barbaradeleo.com and Barbara will be in touch!

ABOUT BARBARA

Multi award winning author, Barbara DeLeo's first book, co-written with her best friend, was a story about beauty queens in space. She was eleven, and the sole, handwritten copy was lost years ago much to everyone's relief. It's some small miracle that she kept the faith and now lives her dream of writing sparkling contemporary romance with unforgettable characters.

Degrees in English and Psychology, and a career as an English teacher, fueled Barbara's passion for people and stories, and a number of years living in Europe —primarily in Athens, Greece—gave her a love for romantic settings.

Discovering she was having her second set of twins in two years, Barbara knew she must be paying penance for being disorganized in a previous life and now uses every spare second to create her stories.With every word she writes, Barbara is sharing her belief in the transformational power of loving relationships.

Married to her winemaker hero for twenty two years, Barbara's happiest when she's getting to know her latest cast of characters. She still loves telling stories about finding love in all the wrong places, but now without a beauty queen or spaceship in sight.

facebook.com/BarbaraDeleoAuthor
twitter.com/BarbDeLeo

A Home for Summer
A Tall, Dark and Driven book
Costa's story
by Barbara DeLeo

This book is a work of fiction. Names, characters, places and incidents are the product of the author's imagination or are used fictitiously. Any resemblance to actual events, locales, or persons, living or dead, is coincidental.

Cover Design - Natasha Snow Designs www.natashasnow.com

available here.

ACKNOWLEDGEMENTS

Not only was I lucky enough to have been born into a wonderfully supportive family where dreams are championed and crazy little quirks celebrated, I've been welcomed into a second family too. Since I met my Greek boyfriend, now husband, thirty years ago, I've been immersed in a culture, a language, and a way of celebrating life that I love. I'd like to thank both families for giving me love, laughter, and inspiration for the story of the Katsalos family in my *Tall, Dark and Driven* series.

My heartfelt thanks also goes to:

My agent, Nalini Akolekar, who always has my back and wonderful advice to share.

My incredible crit partners, Hayson Manning and Rachel Bailey, who are amazing writers and save my patootie time and time again.

Iona, Sue, Kate, Courtney, Deborah and Nadine who are the BEST group of motivators, cheerleaders and wine drinking pals a girl could have.

My cover designer, Natasha Snow, who nails it every time.

My copy editor Elizabeth King whose Type A attention to detail is legendary.

And to George and my four amazing children, thank you for helping me to keep on living this dream. Squeeze, squeeze, squeeze.

Barb X

Printed in Great Britain
by Amazon

62545800R00132